Old friends, like old swords, still are trusted best.

John Webster

Old Swords

And Other Stories

Desmond Hogan

THE LILLIPUT PRESS
DUBLIN

First published 2009 by
THE LILLIPUT PRESS
62–63 Sitric Road, Arbour Hill,
Dublin 7, Ireland
www.lilliputpress.ie

A CIP record for this title is available
from The British Library.

ISBN   978 1 84351 144 1

10 9 8 7 6 5 4 3 2 1

Set in 11.5pt on 13.5pt Centaur by Marsha Swan
Printed in England by Athenaeum Press Ltd, Tyne and Wear

Contents

Old Swords
And Other Stories

Belle

I first made her acquaintance in the cabin the little man who worked on the railway lived in, when I was eleven.

On his wall was an advertisement for Y-fronts based on James Fenimore Cooper's *The Last of the Mohicians* — Hawkeye and Uncas with butch cuts, in Y-fronts, marching alongside one another, with a turkey in long johns bearing a mace on the front of them; a photograph of Cardinal Tien, Archbishop of Peking and exiled Primate of China; Margaret Mitchell in a black antebellum dress with an aigrette of gems at her neck; a photograph of a boy with sideburns in nothing but a peach waisted coat and brothel creepers; and his sterling possession — a postcard of Belle Brinklow, the London music-hall artiste who'd married the young earl of the local manor — red cinnamon hair, heliotrope eyes, mousseline Gibson girl dress with scarlet flannel belt, the words, 'To the Idol of My Heart', underneath.

The manor was now a boys' school and when I started there boys had pudding-bowl Beatles' haircuts and wore dun-and-wine turtleneck jerseys and Australian bush shoes with elasticated sides.

There were three mementoes of the Belle still in the school:

A lunette-shaped daguerreotype of her music-hall colleague, Maude Branscombe, clinging to the Cross of Christ.

A Worcester coffee pot with tulip trees and quail on it she and

Bracebridge, the young earl, used to have their hot chocolate from.

A portrait Sarah Purser did of the Belle when she was working on the stained-glass windows of Loughrea Cathedral nearby — for which the Belle donned her music-hall apparel: shepherdess hat with a demi-wreath of cornflowers, ostrich-feather boa, seed-pearl choker, tea-rose pink dress with double puff sleeves, bouquet of lavender and asters from the autumn garden in her hand.

Belle Brinklow, who was from Bishop's Stortford, used to perform in theatres with names like the Globe, Royal Alfred, Britannia, Surrey, Creswick, Trocadero, Standard, and in sing-song halls of pubs like the Black Horse in Piccadilly and the Cider Cellars in Maiden Lane.

An orchestra in front with brass, woodwind, percussion, a bit of Brussels carpet on the stage, a drop scene of Edinburgh Castle or a Tudor village.

In a Gainsborough hat or a Cossack hat, she'd do the cancan — the Carmagnole of the French Revolution — a handkerchief skirt dance, a barefoot Persian dance or a clog dance; in a Robin Hood jacket, knee breeches, silk stockings, in Pierrot costume, in bell-bottom trousers and coatee she'd sing songs like 'They Call Me the Belle of Dollis Hill' or 'Street Arab Song':

> Out at
> Dawn, nothing got to do.

Then a man in a bat cloak and viridian tights might come on and recite a bit of Shakespeare.

> Now for our Irish wars.
> We must supplant those rough rug-headed kerns,
> Which live like venom ...

One Shakespearean actor who followed her died on stage, in biretta and medieval-cardinal red, reciting Cardinal Wolsey's farewell speech from *Henry VIII*.

Occasionally the Belle teamed up with her sister who was another Belle — who otherwise wore woodland hats — for the purpose of doing leg shows, both of them in winged Mercury hats, tight bodices and gossamer tulle basket skirts with foamy petticoats.

They did matinées at the Gaiety Theatre on the Strand where Ireland's leader Charles Stewart Parnell and the hoydenish Kitty O'Shea, who wore dresses fastened to the neck with acorn buttons, fell in love in a box during a performance in 1880.

The duettists were known to conclude performances with the singing of 'Shepherd of Souls' from *The Sign of the Cross*.

Bracebridge was one of the few men who were allowed backstage.

Others were Lord MacDuff, the Marquess of Anglesey, Sir George Wombwell and the notorious Posno brothers, both of whom were fond of turning up in deerstalkers.

In a Chinese-red waistcoat from Poole's Gentleman's Outfitters, Limerick gloves in hand, cornucopia of golden cockerel hair, eyes the blue of the woodland bugle flower, he came into her dressing room one night and escorted her to Jimmies – the St James Restaurant in Piccadilly.

Afterwards they'd go to the Adelaide Galleries – the Gatti's Restaurant in the Strand or Evan's Song and Supper Rooms where there was a madrigal choir.

She married him in a dragonfly-blue art-nouveau dress with a music-hall corsage of myrtle blossoms in St James's in Piccadilly.

At the end of the nineteenth century and at the beginning of the twentieth there was a craze for music-hall girls to marry into the peerage.

In 1884 Kate Vaughan, star of *Flowers and Words* by Gilbert Hastings McDermott, married Colonel Arthur Frederick Wellesley, son of the Earl of Cowley and nephew of the Duke of Wellington.

Three years after the Belle married Bracebridge, Connie Gilchrist married the Earl of Orkney.

Maud Hobson married a captain of the 11th Hussars and went to Samoa with him where she befriended Robert Louis Stevenson and sang 'Pop Me on the Pier at Brighton' to him while he was dying.

In the mid-nineties, Rosie Boote, the County Tipperary music-hall girl, who was fond of posing in doges' hats, married the Marquess of Headfort and became the Marchioness of Headfort.

At the beginning of the twentieth century Sylvia Lillian Storey became the Countess Poulett; Denise Orme, Baroness Churston;

Olive 'Meatyard' May, Countess of Drogheda; Irene Richards married Lord Drumlanrig.

One music-hall girl was courted by an Italian count who bought her a silvered leopard-skin coat worth three thousand pounds; she ran away with him, he divested her of her coat and she came back to the stage door, begging for work, was sent to music halls in the north, where Jenny Hill used to polish pewter in pubs during the day and sang in the song halls at night before being acclaimed on the London stage.

As late as 1925, Beatrice Lillie married Robert Peel, great-grandson of the prime minister.

Before she left for Ireland, Bracebridge brought the Belle to a production of *The Colleen Bawn* at Her Majesty's in Haymarket, which was about a young lord in the west of Ireland who married a peasant girl, got tired of her and drowned her, the horses refused to cross the bridge to his place of execution and he got out and walked to his own execution.

In the foul-smelling Broadstone Station where they got the train to the west she wore a black riding hat with foxtail feathers and a bear muff, he a Hussar-blue covert coat with brandenbourgs — silk barrel-shaped buttons.

On the terrace of the manor he showed her how the pear and cherry blossom came first, then the apple, then the lilac, then the chestnut and laburnum, the oak last. He indicated the kitten caterpillar, the thrush snail, the speckled wood butterfly, which were abundant because the garden bordered on the woods, approached by the Long Walk.

A year after she arrived in Ireland the Irish clown Johnny Patterson, with whom she frequently appeared on the London stage, was killed during a riot at a circus in Castleisland, County Kerry.

Four years after she came to Ireland her friend, the Belle Daisy Hughes, after a performance at the Brighton Empire, threw herself from the balcony of the Grand Hotel, Brighton, to her death.

The Belle gave two performances in Ireland.

One at the Gaiety Theatre where, shortly after its opening in 1871, Emily Soldene rode a horse on stage in Renaissance pageboy leggings.

In a beefeater-red chiffon dress, trimmed with petals, against a drop scene of Sleepy Hollow in Wicklow, she sang 'When the Happy Time Shall Come' from H.J. Byron's *The Bohemian Girl*, 'The Belle of High Society', 'Molly the Marchioness', 'O, I Love Society', 'Tommy Atkins', 'The Butler Kissed the Housemaid', 'The Footman Kissed the Cook', 'It was a Year Ago', 'Love', 'In the Balmy Summer Time'.

She shared the bill with an underwater acrobatic couple in broadly striped bathing costumes who displayed in a tank, and Nat Emmett's performing goats.

The other was at the Leinster Hall in Hawkins Street where, shortly after it opened as the New Theatre Royal in 1821, a bottle was thrown at the Lord Lieutenant. In the old Theatre Royal in Smock Alley guns were used to clear the audience off the stage.

In a tartan dress and glengarry — a Scottish hat — against a drop scene of Galway docks with swans, she sang 'The Titsy Bitsy Girl', 'Tip I Addy Ay', 'Louisiana Lou', 'Her Golden Hair', 'I saw Esau Kissing Kate', 'Our Lodger's Such a Nice Young Man', 'Maisie is a Daisy', and the oldest vaudeville song, 'Lillibulero', sung by the victors after the Battle of the Boyne, sung in Dublin as part of an all-child cast production of *The Beggar's Opera* in 1729.

On the bill with her were dogs ridden by monkeys in jockey caps and Miss Hunt's possum-faced Ladies' Orchestra, all in bicorne hats and Hussar uniforms, who played Thomas Moore's 'Melodies' to a weeping audience.

Captain O'Shea, Kitty O'Shea's husband, whose mother was a papal countess, had been Member of Parliament for Bracebridge's area, Parnell having endorsed him with a speech in Galway in 1886, and the Bishop of Galway alleged it was a prostituted constituency, in return for Captain O'Shea's connivance in the Parnell–Kitty O'Shea liaison.

When Captain O'Shea finally decided to sue for divorce at the end of 1889, the year the Belle came to Ireland, by all accounts the London music-hall stage had a feast, and the hilarity was compounded by a maid's declaration at the divorce trial that Parnell had once escaped out the window by means of a rope fire escape.

Parnell was represented with a Quaker collar, frock coat, Shetland clown's trousers, hobnail boots. Comediennes wore whalebone corsetting to emphasize Kitty O'Shea's rotundities. Captain O'Shea was usually endowed with an enlarged curlicue moustachio like a Dion Boucicault sheriff.

'Notty Charlie Parnell!' Drop scene painters had a Hibernian spree. One Parnell production featured a Barbary ape in a bowler hat, sealskin waistcoat, trousers embroidered with salad-green shamrocks.

At the end of the 1890s the Belle heard how comedians came on stage in London dressed in prison uniform and their comedienne partners addressed them as 'Oscar' with a flip of the hand.

Lord Alfred Douglas wore a school straw or a domed, wide-brimmed child's hat, Eton jacket with white carnation, drawers, calf stockings, his cheeks the red of a carousel horse's cheeks.

The Prince of Wales, shortly to be Edward VII, an aficionado of the music halls, was said to have turned his back in his box when Lord Alfred Douglas was presented in black-and-pink striped drawers.

But shocked ladies actually left the theatre when he appeared in Jaeger pyjamas with frogged breast buttons.

In 1900 the Belle was one of the ladies who helped serve bon-bonnières to fifteen thousand children in the Phoenix Park on the occasion of the visit by Queen Victoria, a return visit to the city where in 1849 she autographed the Book of Kells.

The Guards Band on the terrace of Windsor Castle were one day playing one of the music-hall songs the Belle used to sing, 'Come where the Booze is Cheap', when Queen Victoria, who was taught singing by Mendelssohn, sent Lady Antrim to find out what the wonderful music was.

The Belle's colleague Kate Vaughan's marriage broke up with Colonel Arthur Frederick Wellesley and she went to Johannesburg where, in elbow gloves on bare arms and a corsage of wild gardenias, she became the Belle of the Gaiety Theatre there. Shortly after she wrote to the Belle about the mauve raintree and the coral tree with cockatoo flowers, she died on a night when Gertie Millar, who was to marry the Earl of Dudley, was playing in one of her roles in *Ali Baba* in London. The Belle had a photograph of her disembarking at Cape Town in a matinée hat.

The owl-like Catholic landlord in neighbouring Loughrea, renowned for promoting boys' choirs, decided to build a new cathedral and the Belle and Bracebridge would often take a brougham there and watch the stained-glass windows being put in, most often speedwell blues, and sometimes at evening the Belle would stand under windows depicting the Ascension and the Last Judgment and recall visits before shows with the French music-hall artiste, Madame Desclause, in her black Second Empire dress, to the Royal Bavarian Church in Piccadilly.

On late-autumn afternoons as they returned from Loughrea the beeches would be old gold and the bushes assaulted to misshape.

A music-hall poster, which depicted a chorus girl holding up a short dress edged in chinchilla-like material, caused clerical outrage in Cork but the clergy were appeased by the king's frequent visits to the music hall, very often in a kilt with a cockade on his stockings. A Dublin music hall caused all-round offence by featuring Admiral Nelson from Nelson's Pillar in Sackville Street with Lady Hamilton in a negligée. The king visited Galway, for the second time in his reign, in gaiters, the Queen in pillar-box red with a Spanish riding hat, a group of Connaught Rangers singing a music-hall song, 'Tara-ra-boom-de-ay', as an anthem for them.

The Belle read *Jane Eyre* bound in red morocco, by Charlotte Brontë, who'd died while pregnant, married to a parson, Arthur Bell Nicholls, and was remembered for walking alone in a *barège* dress by the Shannon.

On the terrace the Belle and Bracebridge would incessantly play on a horn gramophone a Gramophone & Typewriter record of Joseph O'Mara singing 'Friend and Lover', as they had their hot chocolate from a tray with the rose, the thistle, the shamrock. Bracebridge sometimes took an opera hat to Kilkee in the summer where they had listened to the German band on the boardwalk. The gilt and cranberry theatres of Dublin magneted with pantomimes – *Jack and the Beanstalk*, *Puss in Boots*, *Aladdin* and *Princess Badroulboudour*.

There was a brief visit to Belgium where they looked at a Rubens painting. Auburn moustachio. Watermelon-pink cleavage. Plumed hat. Boy with peach slashings on his arms. Cirrus horse. Despite the smiles the sky tells you that war is near.

The Belle was one of the ladies' committee who saw the Connaught Rangers off from the North Wall in August 1914, with chocolates and madeleines.

The swallows in the eaves had a second brood that year and didn't leave until October. When the alders were in white, pulpy berry on either side of the Forty Steps at the end of the Long Walk she'd go there, stand on top of the steps, sing her music-hall songs lest they be stamped out in her.

Soldiers camped in the demesne and at night sang 'It's a Long Way to Tipperary', which the Melbourne music-hall girl, Florrie Forde, who ran away when she was fourteen, used to sing, the words printed an inch high at the footlights so thousands could join in.

A late Indian summer visit to Kilkee — dramatic mare's tails in the morning sky, a dense fruit of bindweed flowers on the bushes, ladybirds doing trapeze acts on withered fleabane, the late burnet roses becoming clusters of black berries, a dolphin thrashing in the horseshoe bay, a coloratura rendition of 'Take, Oh Take Those Lips Away' from *The Bohemian Girl* at an evening get-together by a man with a Vandyke beard when news came that the mail boat was sunk just after leaving Kingston Harbour, with the loss of five hundred lives.

During the War of Independence, from a window, over bonfires at night or under the ornamental crab-apple tree or the weeping-pear tree in the garden she could hear the soldiers sing songs from the music halls: 'On Monday I Walked Out with a Soldier', 'The Girl the Soldiers Always Leave Behind Them', 'All Through Sticking to a Soldier', 'Aurelia was Always Fond of Soldiers', 'Soldiers of the Queen', but especially, 'Soldiers in the Park', which was where they were, burning leaves.

When the Black and Tans raced up and down Sackville Street in vans covered in wire and there was a curfew, she was one of Dublin's few theatre-goers, taking the tram from a house in Dalkey to Harcourt Street Station, which replaced summer bivouacs in Morrison's Hotel in Dawson Street, in a taffeta hobble skirt tied near the ankle with sash lace, so that the horrible hobble of British taste made her less likely to be a target.

It was commonplace in those days to see Countess Markievicz, the minister for labour in the revolutionary government, cycling around Dublin on a battered bicycle, in a beehive bonnet from which cherries dangled. Her sister, Eva Gore Booth, had devoted part of her life in England to the rights of women music-hall artistes.

The need to perform overcame her because she sang 'Goo-Goo' from *The Earl and the Girl* at a concert in the Theatre Royal, Limerick, spring 1922, in aid of those made homeless by the War of Independence. She was photographed on that occasion outside Joseph O'Mara's house, Hartstonge House — Eton-crop hair now, pumps with Byzantine, diamanté buckles.

The Belle and Bracebridge were in St Nicholas's Cathedral in Galway in early summer 1922, to see the colours of the Connaught Rangers, the harp and crown on yellow, which dated back to 1793, being removed, on the first stage of their journey to Windsor Castle.

At the beginning of 1923, during the Civil War, the Belle started out two days early, defying derailed trains and broken bridges, joining hordes from his native Athlone to hear John McCormack singing 'The Last Rose of Summer' in a black cloak lined with ruby silk, at a home-visit concert.

Near the Forty Steps that spring, with its bloody cranesbill and its blue cranesbill, she found an abandoned blackbird's nest, covered in moss.

There were ladybird roundabouts in the Fair Green when she and Bracebridge left, childless, to live in a Queen Anne revival lodge near the red-brick Victorian Gothic church of St Chad's in Birmingham, but not before she was received into the Roman Catholic Church, under a portrait of Cardinal Wiseman in garnet red, in the local church, joining the faith of a London music-hall Belle who claimed to be related to Father Prout the poet, a Cork priest who penned 'The Bells of Shandon', rowed with his native city, was an associate of Charles Dickens and W.M. Thackeray, mixed his priestly duties with the bohemian life, travelled as far as Hungary and Asia Minor, with his Latin translations of the songs of Thomas Moore was a leading attraction at Mrs Jameson's Sunday evening parties in Rome and ended up with his rosary and psalm book in a mezzanine in Paris.

The manor was sold to priests; there were people cycling on the Suck that winter it was so cold, and the priests came and taught Thucydides.

One of the *inculabula* that survived the transaction, which instilled fear in the boys, especially at Lent, was one with an illustration of Caroline of Brunswick in a celestial blue dress, with matching jacket edged in swan's down, and a high-crowned Eliza-bethan gentleman's hat, banging on the doors of Westminster Cathe-dral during the coronation of George IV in 1820, demanding to be allowed in as the Queen of England, the doors barred against her.

It joined the books that the priests favoured, which were books with illustrations by Arthur Rackham so that boys going to the school got a vision of life with boys in bathing costumes and girls in dresses with sailor's trim by the tide's edge; New York streets crowded with pigs in derby hats or cloche hats; women in mob caps cherishing their babies in clapboard New England towns; couples enshrined in four-poster beds with rose-motif curtains; bare-footed girls carrying bundles wrapped in peacock-eye patterned cloth through fox-coloured forests; ancient Irish heroes in togas doing marathon runs; small boys in glove-fitting short trousers stomping on plethoric daisies; bare-breasted Rhine maidens in Heimkunst rites.

Just before I left England I visited a man in Bath who'd been a student in the school during the Second World War when a song the Belle sang, 'Maisie is a Daisy', was revived and sung on radio by Maidie Andrews alongside Gracie Fields' 'So I'm Sending a Letter to Santa Claus to Bring Daddy Safely Home to Me'.

A Palladian square of the Adam style, façade breaking into towers.

A man with a Noah beard in the green, brown and off-white of the Epicurean Graigian sect on it.

A room with lyres, garlands, acanthus on the walls.

A man with mud-green eyes, hirsute brows, in a lap robe, reflected in a photograph of a Beau Brummell of the Irish midlands in a striped beach jacket and cricket shirt.

Christmas 1943, shortly after Churchill, Stalin and Roosevelt met in Teheran, he played Fifi, in Salvation Army fatigues, in *The Belle of New York* at the school, having played Prudence in *The Quaker Girl* the year before and Countess Angela in *The Count of Luxembourg*.

The production was directed by a priest who'd seen the new pope, Eugenio Pacelli, being hailed with the Nazi salute by German boy scouts, summer 1939. He'd caught a swim in the shock-cerulean Mediterranean in Portovenere, where Byron used to swim, on the day the German–Soviet Non-Aggression Pact was signed.

As Fifi, the man I visited had to sing 'Teach me How to Kiss, Dear', a song that became popular in the rugby changing rooms.

The priest-director commented that he was an annual reminder that the Emporer Nero had married a boy.

Each night when Blinky Bill — who had a slight goat's moustache and was fond of quoting 'Tragedy is true Guise. Comedy lies,' from his schoolteacher father in Creggs, County Galway, where Parnell made his last rain-soaked speech — sang 'She is the Belle of New York', the ghost of the Belle could be seen in the wings in a harem-scarem skirt — a skirt with cuffed and buttoned ankles like Turkish pantaloons — summer sombrero, music-hall, droplet earrings under shingled hair.

Iowa

At a booth table in a bar in Iowa, a nearby field of early Quaker graves, stones with no name on them, under snow, an exile from Clare, in an Eskimo parka, who teaches students, some of them as tall as Arthur Rimbaud, over a rainbow-rayed cocktail, told me, during a brief stopover on a Greyhound bus journey, about the colossus of a garda sergeant with earthed barley-sugar hair and eyes that were the grey-blue of his uniform – a goalkeeper who'd won six gold medals – who used to cycle a Darley Peterson of army green to a remote rocky swimming place in Clare during the Second World War and seduce the boys among the white thrift, the bird's-foot trefoil, the kidney vetch, the white rock roses, the *buachalán* – ragwort – the scarlet pimpernel, a brief Dionysian dispensation about this place – boys with lobster-coloured body hair holding broadcloth shorts or knit briefs or olive-drab briefs with V-notches to themselves in a moirdered way, while a harem of lamenting seals looked on.

The man returned one winter from his university in Iowa, where he had a girlfriend, who wore glitter jodhpur boots, who'd lived in a monkey colony in the mountains before fleeing the Chinese Revolution, with whom he went to look at the Colombian sharp-tailed grouse and the whooping cranes, and revisited the swimming place – the boys in the nearby town in their laurel-green school jackets like the boys from Plato's *Symposium* now — a few cubicles newly built with a lifebuoy alongside them, a porpoise thrashing in the mica of sleet in the winter rain.

In a local speakeasy he'd been told the story of how the paediatrician widow of a Royal Irish Constabulary inspector, murdered in County Wexford in 1920, after his death presented a painting she'd purchased in Edinburgh to the Jesuit community in Dublin and that recently the painting was discovered to have been by Caravaggio who loved painting boys.

> If I take the wings of the morning, and dwell in the uttermost
>   parts of the sea;
> Even there shall thy hand lead me, and thy right hand shall
>   hold me.

Frederick Rolfe, Baron Corvo, took photographs of naked Italian boys.

But the garda sergeant took photographs of naked Irish boys and had them developed by an accomplice in Ennis, where the Code of the Irish Constabulary had been printed in 1820.

Boys with rousse-auburn hair and cranberry pubic hair. Walnut hirsute. Heron's features or faces like young kangaroos. Some with hair the orange of the pheasant in ascent. Others with Creole curls. Many with identical passion-fruit lips.

Frequently a Woodbine cigarette in the mouth of a nude. A few of them reclining like lizards. One or two in yachting caps like the man on the Player's cigarette packet and nothing else.

There were nudes in sunglasses. Nudes with Lucania bicycles. Nudes with hurleys.

It was hurling in east Clare and football in west Clare and it was mainly footballers he photographed.

Very occasionally there were Falstaffian interlopers from Garryowen and St Mary's rugby teams in Limerick.

A man who teaches in the Gothic St Flannan's College in Ennis still has a photograph taken by the garda sergeant.

Boy with pompadour quiff, in belted scoutmaster shorts, standing against the rocks where frogs live in abundance, hands on the rocks, his chest thrown forward, Lana Turner-style.

It was not forgotten in County Clare that during the War of Independence, in Dublin, some boys shot British agents in their beds, some beside their wives.

Then, as they were being searched for in the city, they played a football match. A few of those boys later went mad and ended up in mental homes.

Michael Cusack himself, who'd founded the Gaelic Athletic Association in 1884, was from Carron in County Clare.

It had never been forgotten that shortly after the Irish defeat at the Battle of the Boyne in County Meath, where Gaelic football was particularly popular and used be followed by wrestling, some Wexford men crossed to Cornwall, tied yellow ribbons around their waists to distinguish themselves, and trounced the Cornish men at hurling.

Nor was it forgotten that after the Battle of the Boyne the victors had sung 'The Protestant Boys', composed by the Marquis of Wharton, frequently sung by Lord Byron's friend, the County Clare poet Thomas Dermody, as 'Lillibulero'.

The Gaelic Athletic Association spread like prairie fire in the years just after its foundation, Michael Cusack said.

One of the first football teams used flour bags as jerseys.

The Gaelic Athletic Association turned up en masse to Parnell's funeral in 1891, to which his widow in Brighton, Kitty O'Shea, was afraid to go.

On the day the Second World War broke out Kilkenny was playing Cork in hurling in Dublin, a day of thunder and lightning and rain, Kilkenny winning with a decisive point from a man from Castleshock.

Roscommon won the All-Ireland football final that month.

Often the Clare boys went to Ballinasloe to play games, where the football star Michael Knacker Walsh was from, staying in the workhouse, singing 'The West Clare Express' in the showers: 'It spends most of its time off the track.'

Connaught finals were played in St Coman's Park in Roscommon and these were a treat because the people of Roscommon town opened their houses as guesthouses for the occasions and served spice cake and butterfly buns at their hall doors.

People converged on the town in thousands on bicycles for these occasions.

At the end of September some of the Clare boys journeyed to Dublin, staying in the Grand Hotel, Malahide, to see the All-Ireland football final for a cup modelled on the Ardagh Chalice.

On these visits to Dublin it was mandatory, in suits with long jackets and padded chests, to call in on the all-day cartoon show in the rich-crimson, basement Grafton Cinema, which sold claret, port, rum and champagne gums in the foyer, and to admire the interlaced roundels and the floriated scrollwork of the Book of Kells in Trinity College.

A few of them went to a production of *The Duchess of Malfi* at the Gate Theatre in which all the actors wore hearse-cloth costumes.

> O, this gloomy world.
> In what a shadow, or deep pit of darkness,
> Doth womanish and fearful mankind live!

The garda sergeant was a great fan of John McCormack and in the barracks at night on a gramophone he'd play John McCormack singing Don Ottavio in *Don Giovanni*, Rachmaninoff's 'When Night Descends', Handel's 'Tell Fair Irene', Earl Bristol's 'Farewell', 'The Short Cut to the Rosses', 'The Snowy Breasted Pearl', 'Green Grows the Laurel', Villiers Stanford's 'Lament for Owen Roe O'Neill'.

He himself was known to sing the renowned ballad, 'The Peeler and the Goat', about a drunken goat who was impounded by an Irish Constabulary officer in County Tipperary.

In the nineteen-thirties and -forties, while the rest of Ireland suffered, it was common to have garda sergeants who were libertine or even bohemian.

Garda Sergeant Clohessy was from Galway city and, in the extreme viridian of Galway before it changed to maroon and white and in snowflake-white calf stockings, used to play football with the Kilconierin team.

In the years just after independence, his hair Rudolph Valentino-style, he went to train as a guard in the Phoenix Park Depot, where sick members of the Royal Irish Constabulary used to wear bottle blue to distinguish themselves from the rifle green of their healthy colleagues, sleeping on a triple bedboard.

He began taking photographs of other garda recruits in woollen-bib swimming costumes with striped trim on the trousers of the trunks on Jameson's Beach in Howth with a Wollensak camera.

He was among two hundred and fifty pilgrim gardaí, whose organization had been founded in the Gresham Hotel, Dublin, shortly after the Treaty, who travelled to Rome in the autumn of 1928, met at the umber Rome Central by the staff and students of the Irish College, parading to lay a wreath on the Tomb of the Unknown Soldier, wearing medals with the cradle-blue ribbons of pilgrimage on their uniforms with buckram-stiffened high necks, addressed and lauded by Pius XI whose predecessor Pius X, on the occasion of his jubilee, had been entertained with bagpipes by the son of a County Galway Royal Irish Constabulary officer, in full kilted uniform, shown the paintings of the Vatican Gallery by a priest from the Irish College; the carmines, the damasks, the logan-berries, the coral reds, the cyclamen red, the rose reds of the *St Jerome of Francesco Mola*, the *St Jerome* of Girolamo Muziano, the *Deposition of Christ* by Caravaggio, *The Vision of St Helena* by Veronese, the *Martyrdom of St Erasmus* by Poussin.

But it was the statue of Caesar Augustus with his double fore-lock and parade armour, which attracted the most attention, who, the priest told them, put a serpent nearly ninety feet long in front of the Domitium and decreed crossroad gods should be crowned twice a year, with spring and summer flowers.

Back in Galway, stationed in Eglinton Street Barracks, he won his medals, playing in places like Parkmore, Tuam and Cusack Park, Mullingar, wearing a Basque beret on the field.

The Galway team had a trainer then, who used to cut pictures

of Greek gods out of books and frame them, who'd take them to
Tuam where they'd stay in Canavan's Hotel and eat lashings of
boiled potatoes.

He'd have them run for miles as far as Greenfield where they'd
jump into Lough Corrib.

In 1934 Garda Clohessy travelled with the Galway team on the
Manhattan to the United States, sighted the petrel known to sailors as
Mother Carey's chicken in the eastern Atlantic, heard Guido Cic-
colini who'd sung at Rudolph Valentino's funeral.

The former commissioner of the guards, who'd been received
by Benito Mussolini and a goose-stepping cohort during the pilgrimage of 1928, relieved of his post earlier that year by Mr de
Valera, had become leader of the Irish Fascist Movement in 1933.

In November 1936 five hundred of the Irish fascists turned up
in Galway to sail for Spain and fight for Franco.

Thirty-four of them had a last-minute change of mind and
turned back.

Two of the Irish fascists were shot on their arrival in Spain by
Franco's men because of their strange uniform.

When a French actor in a greatcoat, known in Galway for his
performance as a French revolutionary murdered in a bath, was
giving street performances in Eyre Square in September 1937, Garda
Clohessy was promoted to sergeant, given a uniform with chevrons
of silver braid on the sleeve, and transferred to Clare.

Ned Hannaford's circus was playing on his arrival; an entrée act
of a giraffe-necked woman in gold-leaf brassiere and trunks on a
Suffolk Punch horse followed by United States cavalrymen; Poodles
Hannaford in a leopard-skin loincloth driving six Rosinback horses
of flea-bitten hue tandem, standing astride; a brief scene from
Shakespeare's *Midsummer-Night's Dream* accompanied by Catherine
wheels … 'kill me a red-hipped humble-bee on the top of a thistle';
pigmy African elephants waited upon by baboons in frock coats.

In Rome Garda Sergeant Clohessy had been told by the priest
from the Irish College how Lucius Aemilius Paullus had deserters in
the war against Perseus trampled to death by elephants in the Circus
Flaminius.

An English fair used to come to the town, where some of the

houses were painted Wallis Warfield Simpson blue, each year before the war and the gaff boys, many with the common features of Venetian-blonde hair – dark mottled with blonde – and dead-white lips, and wearing costume rings, used to swim in the swimming hole.

It was these that Garda Sergeant Clohessy started his nude photography on, with a Voigtlander Prominent.

Some of the local boys left with the fair and themselves stood around the dodgems and gondolas and ghost trains as gaff boys in places like St Briavels in Gloucestershire.

The Clare Champion featured one of the garda sergeant's earliest efforts, that of a football star from Fedamore in County Limerick, with auburn cockscomb, eyes the blue of the gentians that grew in places where wintering cattle had curtailed the hazel trees, after some triumph.

What *The Clare Champion* didn't know was that at the football game at Killarn the garda sergeant photographed the football star, with the chest of an Eros the Spartans used sacrifice to before going to war, in shorts with gripper fasteners on Dunbeg beach, the youth's hands on his crotch, against the sea, which was the colour of shillings that magpies would steal, on a day the Irish leaders de Valera, Cosgrave and Norton took their seats at a pro-neutrality rally in Dublin, and afterwards, without his shorts, lying face down, among the purple saxifrage of the dunes.

To ease his reservations Garda Sergeant Clohessy cited the mature *Apollo Belvedere*, naked but with a *paludamentum* – cloak – the *Belvedere Torso* on panther skin that had inspired Michelangelo, the boy who combats naked with a goose, Bernini's near-naked *Daniel* with sideswept, cricket-boy hair, all in the Vatican Gallery.

A youth from South Hill in Limerick, ash-blonde hair and barley-coloured freckles, his left nostril murdered, cut away in a pub brawl, was among those photographed.

Hands in the black bog rush, legs provocatively apart, head thrown back in abandon.

As the Allies were landing in Sicily and there were riots in Hollywood, some girls with braids like Pippi Longstocking arrived in the swimming hole but they were chased away with a stick by the garda sergeant.

People came to the sea on donkeys and carts then; crubeens – pigs' feet – were proffered for a penny. There was a café near the main beach run by an immense Italian man, which sold sea bass, soft cod's roe.

An American film about Charles Stewart Parnell starring Clark Gable and Myrna Loy was brought from Limerick in cans and shown in the parochial hall, where there were photographs of Pope Pius XII and of Cardinal Franz von Galen von Löwe of Münster, and afterwards the garda sergeant's boys mingled with the holiday-making girls from Limerick, many of them wearing flared linen trousers, and led some of them to the fields, which were a festival of orchids.

Tramming the hay, building cocks of hay it was called then, and Christian Brothers, on leave from schools around Ireland, were employed to tram the hay.

Garda Sergeant Clohessy even convinced a Christian Brother with cowslip-coloured hair and eyes the blue of the Peloponnesos where the two seas meet, to pose in the nude.

A boy with a sea-cow belly took a photograph of Garda Sergeant Clohessy and in it he looks like Caesar Augustus: Roman nose; accentuated, slightly feminine lips; pennon neck; cauliflower ears.

The previous June he'd been photographed leading the Corpus Christi procession through the town, women in coats with large collar-revers and boxy shoulders immediately behind him.

Someone had put a bunch of cornflowers in front of a nearby shrine that told: 'My name is Jeremiah Marriman. I built this shrine in thanksgiving for being cured. Also for my son Loughlin. Thanks be to God and Our Blessed Lady' – red, orange and white plastic flowers in front of a picture of Thérèse of Lisieux, a little statue of Christ beside a black snail with citron rings.

The Spanish Armada ship *San Esteban* had floundered in the vicinity and its crew did not suffer the fate of the Spanish Armada ship whose crew had been massacred by Dowdarra Roe O'Malley in County Mayo, but had married in the neighbourhood and sometimes when Garda Sergeant Clohessy took a photograph he was confronted by an ebony-haired boy from the land of El Greco who, if he wasn't painting portraits, was conducting lawsuits.

Cromwellian soldiers had chopped off the head of a monk in the uplands where the hen harrier preyed on young rabbits and young hares.

Sometimes when he photographed he was photographing boys with burnt-orange hair and Wedgwood-blue eyes who were descended from soldiers from the English midlands.

Goats came down the slope and looked as he was photographing some boys from Limerick city with Marlovian grins and lamp-black hair who would hang about the truck stop at Harvey's Quay in blanket trousers and seersucker shirts and stand under the trees in Arthur's Quay Park at night or sit late at night in the Treaty Café.

In deference to the goats who were present the garda sergeant sang a bit of his song about the goat:

'"Oh, Mercy Sir," the goat replied, "and let me tell my story-o."'

The Emperor Heliogabalus had been a teenager, he told them, wearing long purple Phoenician garments, embroidered in gold; linen shoes, necklaces, jewels, rouging his cheeks and painting his eyes, appointing actors to the most important posts in the Empire, murdered with his mother Soaemias, by his own soldiers and their bodies thrown into a sewer that ran into the Tiber.

But it was generally agreed that the garda sergeant's most beautiful model was a Jewish refugee from Prague with doe-like limbs who lived in the town for a few years during the war.

'This is what we fought and died for,' the naked garda sergeant greeted the boy on his first arrival at the swimming hole in riding breeches, golf stockings and a thistle dicky bow – a bow with flaps that opened out at both ends – when the comfrey was in white bloom on the sea slopes, before it turned blue.

Father Coughlin's broadcasts in the USA against the Jews were famous in Ireland.

The boy could talk to the garda sergeant about Boccherini, and about Mozart who'd sojourned in a Naples-yellow house in Prague.

The boy's family had brought a reproduction of a painting with them from Prague, which they put in the hall of their house where his mother, who wore culottes as she partook in table quizzes with the local women, made plaited challah bread; a little boy in grey and he had the same polo-pony features as the Jewish boy.

Black bow tie with white polka dots, Eton collar, double-breasted grey suit, straw hat in right hand, toy Pomeranian biting hat, a little greenery behind the boy, left hand in pocket, straw-blonde Eton crop, forget-me-not-blue eyes, prince's apricot smirk.

The boy's hand accidentally touched a gull's egg, light olive with spots of umber, as he was being photographed.

A boy who had been used to a bathing establishment on the Elbe in an Irish summer; a towel slung over one shoulder like a Roman exomis.

The chough lived here – the crow with red legs – a raven lived near here, the natterjack toad – yellow stripe down his back – roamed here. Gannets frequently made passage by the swimming hole.

A light bib-top, which is usually joined with a zip to dark trunks but the trunks removed – fire-red body hair.

At night the boy would go to the garda station with cherry-and-sultana sponge cakes his mother had made and tea would be served on a tray with the Guinness pelican in the penetralia of the garda station, which was dominated by a framed picture of Venus with Adonis's naked leg wrapped around her and he and Garda Sergeant Clohessy would listen to 'Song of the Seals', 'Farewell and Adieu to You', 'Sweet Spanish Ladies', 'So We'll Go No More A-Roving'.

As a trainee guard in Dublin, Garda Sergeant Clohessy had heard how a lock of Byron's hair in a locket had been lost in Kildare Street and he cut off a curl of the Czech boy's hair as a keepsake.

Lord Byron had loved John Edleston more than any human being.

The boy left with his family to live in a house with Virginia creeper on it, which was the red of splodges on a baby's bottom, in the autumn, when de Gaulle entered Paris, but not before he told a Jewish story to the gathering at the swimming hole, a torch of monbretia on the slope above, about a migratory bird with feathers so beautiful they were never seen before, who came for the winter and built his nest at the top of the tallest cedar, how the king ordered a human ladder to be built to the top of the tree so that the bird and his nest could be brought to him, but the people at the bottom of the ladder grew impatient because it was taking so long and broke away so that the ladder collapsed and the bird was never inspected.

On his arrival in Dublin the boy sent the garda sergeant a postcard of an Eros with flashing forget-me-not-blue eyes, in a wolfskin surcoat, playing a flute.

The parenthesis lasted until the end of the war when two nuns picking burnet roses for the Feast of St Colmcille saw a naked man with naked boys washing themselves with Pears' and Lifebuoy soap.

A stamp featuring Douglas Hyde, the first Protestant president of Ireland, was omnipresent at the time and Des Fretwell and his Twelve Piece Orchestra played at the Queens Hotel in Ennis.

The nuns were stronger than the garda sergeant and swiftly got word to a superior and the garda sergeant was transferred to a border county, where the football team wore ox-blood red, when Lord Haw Haw who was from the Lough Corrib country of north Galway, who'd disparaged the naval vessel *Muirchu* on German radio in a nasal voice the result of a broken nose at school, was executed in Wandsworth Prison, and more or less never heard of again except for a sighting by some Claremen who'd accompanied Canon Hamilton of Clare at the Polo Grounds, home of a baseball team, when on the only occasion ever, for the centenary of the Great Famine of 1847, the All-Ireland football final was played outside Ireland.

He was also fleetingly seen at the Commodore Hotel afterwards among the swing dancers, in a hat with the crown flattened into pork-pie shape, with a young man who had a butch cut.

Others said he was sighted on Jones Beach, Long Island, where Walt Whitman used go with an eighteen-year-old Irish boy, Peter

Doyle, to look at the sea fowl, in 1949, which would lead one to believe he decided to settle in the United States.

A garda sergeant in Ennis, a vigilant agent for the Censorship of Publications Board, ambushed Garda Sergeant Clohessy's friend in Ennis, leaping out of hens' and chickens' shrubbery at him, and seized a major part of Garda Sergeant Clohessy's archives, which also included a picture of Johnny Weissmuller as Tarzan, Maureen O'Sullivan as Jane, a golden-haired boy-child and an ape seated on the branch of a tree, and they were never seen again.

From the end of the war people dared only swim in the swimming hole in full regalia, except for an English painter with a Vandyke beard, who'd sit on the rocks in nothing but a rag hat and who referred to the sea by the Greek word *thalassa*.

Young married Traveller boys, many with hair dyed sow-thistle yellow, meet in the town now the first week of August each year, parking their caravans by a football field or on a cliff head, swimming together last thing each evening in the swimming hole in mini-bikini briefs, or boxer shorts with Fiorentina players, or cerulean moons, or in cowboy-faded denim shorts, joining the elderly men who come here in safari shorts, ankle socks, baseball caps, before they move their English-registered caravans to the Killorglin Puck Fair.

Red Tide

Tonight is the night of the Red Tide – St Valentine's Day. Nutrients from inland, with the change of season, after rainy weather, light up the combers, blue and white.

For some days patisserie windows have been full of pralines – cakes composed of mousse, caramel and pecan nuts. Earlier there were boys on skateboards on the boardwalk, in Bermuda shorts with busbies or traveller's cheques on them, carrying bunches of Greek windflowers. Groups of old ladies in owl-eye glasses, in the ruby lake of Mickey Mouse or the lemon of Donald Duck, paraded by the ocean.

An elderly man in a Borsalino hat passed a shaven-headed Chinese boy, with a birthmark on his face like a great burn, who was staring at a flock of plovers, and I thought of shirts I'd worn in London as if they'd been women I'd known – a long-sleeved terracotta shirt with sepia roosters, a short butterfly-sleeved vermilion shirt with coral-grey swallows.

'How do you get to Amsterdam? You take a bus through Ranelagh.' I had this dream shortly before I went to Amsterdam for the first time.

I went with Rena. We were going to travel south from there. In London before setting off we went to an Andy Warhol double bill and all the beautiful, naked young men inspired a greater intensity in our love-making.

We stayed with a Dutch couple we'd met while hitchhiking that summer in north Connemara, on Gerard Doustraat. In the window of the corner café, despite the fact that it was late September, there was a Santa Claus with a hyacinthine beard with little acorns on it.

The couple gave us kipper soup for supper and the following morning we had breakfast cake. On our one full day in Amsterdam we purchased two dozen or so postcards of Jan Mankes paintings and drawings to send to friends. A few self-portraits of Mankes. One in a tiny Roman collar and smock, with a wing quiff, against a lemon landscape. Hair sometimes brown, sometimes amber. Eyes sometimes blue, sometimes brown. A woman in silhouette tending geese. A woman with head dipped in a gaslit room. Salmon-coloured roofs. An old person with a nose like a root vegetable. Birds in snow. An art-nouveau, besequined turkey. A landscape breaking into water. A bunch of honesty. A mouse in the snow. Geese with their beaks to heaven. Goats looking as if they're wearing clogs. A rattan chair. A nightingale. A kestrel. A thrush. An owlet. A reading boy. Birch trees.

It was as if these cards and their images by a painter who'd died young, held together, before being dispatched, on a day when cyclists held golf-sized umbrellas, composed our lives as they had been together.

In Paris we slept near the statue of Henry IV on Pont Neuf.

Then we hitchhiked south. We had an ugly row when we reached the warmth but then a truck took us and brought us as far as Marseille where we both had our first sight of the Mediterranean, cerulean-ash.

The grapes were translucent, hands reaching under them. The hills of Provence were vertigo at evening, little stone walls like the west of Ireland, Roman ruins.

A truck driver with a moustache took us to Monaco where he put us up for the night in an apartment looking to the sea, gave Rena a T-shirt with Gerd Müller of Bayer Leverkusen soccer team on it.

Our first day in Italy we had pasta in a workers' café in the suburbs of Milan, given to us by a blonde waitress in black.

In Venice Rena's face, with her silver-blonde hair and starling's egg-blue eyes, was reflected in glass just blown in a little canalside glass-making place. Her life, her anxieties were in those reflections; a French schoolboy's cape, autumn leaves in Dublin, mustard-coloured leaves lining the long avenue.

We did not stay in the Excelsior Hotel on the Lido. We slept in a large cement pipe but we took advantage of the cordoned-off beaches around the Excelsior. Last effigies of beauty on these beaches in the faltering sunshine of Fall – boys in hi-waist bathing togs.

On the way back we took a tram through the narrow streets of La Spezia, then walked by the apricot, papaya, yellow-ochre-coloured houses of Portovenere to the rocky place where the Harrow muti-neer, Byron, used to swim.

Perhaps it was the light or the lack of sleep but I saw a child there, a little boy in a blue-and-white striped T-shirt.

Rena went back to Dublin from London. I stayed in a house in Hanwell with a reproduction of Arthur Rackham's young Fionn on the wall.

Later in the Fall I ventured to Italy again. Mustard-coloured leaves were reflected in the front mirror of a truck heading towards Florence.

In the Uffizi a Japanese girl with bobbed hair, in a long skirt and high heels with bevelled undersides paused in front of Botti-celli's young man in a skullcap holding a honey-coloured medallion.

On a day trip to Siena I sent a postcard reproduction to Dublin of a self-portrait Dürer did at twenty-two, red tasselled cap, carrying field eryngo in his hand. *Mannstreu* in German meaning man's fidelity.

I saw the turbaned ancient Eygptian Hermes Trismegistus in a pavement mosaic at the entrance to the cathedral.

In Viareggio where the drowned Shelley was cremated with salt and frankincense in the flame, the sky was grey, there were tankers at sea, gold lace on the combers. I swam on the beach there. The grey lifted shortly after Viareggio.

In Rome the skies were cerulean. I paused in front of Pope John XXIII's pilgrim door, I saw the statue of a young, early Christian shepherd with corkscrew curls, I saw a mural Mussolini had com-missioned depicting Odysseus embracing his son Telemachus, I sat in the sunshine near the persimmon throat of a fountain, I listened to Bob Dylan's 'A Satisfied Mind' under the statue of Giordano Bruno.

That statue spoke years later. I read somewhere that he'd said: 'Through the light which shines in the crocus, the daffodil, the sunflower, we ascend to the life that presides over them.'

One night when I slept in a train by Rome's pre-war brown station I was beaten up and everything I had robbed. I had to return to England with a document the Irish embassy gave me and some money my father sent me.

An English girl on the train gave me a jersey of kingfisher blue. The sea was harebell blue at Folkstone. I was stopped by the police. The English girl stood with me.

Back in Dublin at Christmas I found Rena was having an affair with a boy with a Henry-VIII horseshoe beard.

I started teaching in the New Year in a school where a boy brought an Alsatian dog one day, where a prostitute used come into the yard and sing a Dublin courtship song: '... And I tied up me sleeve to buckle her shoe.'

At Easter Rena and I were travelling again together. We had a camera and in Cork, outside Frank O'Connor's cottage, where a woman neighbour had chased an anti-Parnellite priest with a stick, we were photographed and little boys, many of them, arrived out of nowhere and posed behind us, cheering. It was as if they were cheering on my own stories. The roll of film was lost.

The previous Easter we'd stayed in a cottage one weekend in Ballinskelligs with a photograph of a young man in a zoot suit, kipper tie, wingtip shoes, on the wall.

The following weekend, Easter weekend, I returned to Kerry alone and swam in olive-drab underpants in the turquoise water at Clogher Strand.

In the summer we camped near a cliff-side barracks in Duncannon in County Wexford and mutually flirted with the soldiers.

Rena had gone to school in the west of Ireland in a school with a picture of a Penal Days' Mass on the wall, and bits of information from an erudite old nun there were always breaking through her conversation.

'Lord Cornwallis who suppressed the Rising of 1798 had previously lived in Yorktown – New York.'

Near Enniscorthy we picked up a boy in a tiger-stripe tank top and hipster jeans and he slept in the tent with us and after I'd made love to Rena my hand touched his chest.

Some weeks after our trip to Cork bombs went off in Dublin and shortly afterwards Rena went to California.

In October 1976 I went to California from Dublin to see her. In the evening at San Francisco airport her eyes were the blue of a bunch of chicory. She wore a long scarlet skirt surviving from Connemara days. I gave her an old edition of a book by Kate O'Brien. Inside was a motif of swans.

The following afternoon on a boat on San Francisco Bay she asked me about death, mortality. She'd joined a religious group.

We hitchhiked north together, staying in a motel in Mendocino. I'd been working with a street-theatre group in Dublin.

She wore a honeycombed swimsuit. The whales were going south, a *passeggiata* on the horizon.

There was a great palm tree on the beach, maybe the last one north. The distant whales and the morning ultramarine of the Pacific were framed by rocks on either side of the beach as if it was a theatre scene.

She returned to Dublin the following May. The last time I made love to her easily there was an image of Mexican forests in my mind. At a party in Dublin, in front of everyone, a girl accused me of impotence and after that I couldn't make love to Rena anymore. Rena returned to California.

Years later in southern California a boy in a lumber jacket with mailbox pockets would explain the nature of schizophrenia to me – people say things or do things that have no connection with their emotions, with what they feel.

In the summer in southern Egypt, near where some of the Gnostic Gospels were found, Coptic priests in flowing black robes among the little white houses, iron Coptic crosses nearby in the desert, I swam in the Nile, despite the fact that I was warned that there were insects in it that could get into your blood. The Nile was an earthenware-jar cerulean.

I was feeling dead after the attack in Dublin. I walked out into the night in southern Egypt. There were great palm trees against the stars and distantly a man on a camel moved in the desert. In the desert night there were strange sounds, almost songs, half-chants by male voices. There was nothing to distinguish the scene from two thousand years ago. That night I decided to live.

Next morning I went for a swim in the Nile again. There were a few little boys paddling in nappy-like garments. No other swimmers.

On the way back north I visited an Irish poet on a Greek island whose address I'd been given in Dublin. On his hall stand was a Spanish hat.

There were dances on the island in a dance venue that was covered but with open sides. Young men in glove-fitting jeans and girls in white party dresses stood around. The instruments were shot gold and the band played the summoning mariache music of a village afternoon gala. Priests drank coffee by tables that were covered in chequered red and white.

Sophisticated Americans, in bush shirts belted below the waist or cheesecloth peasant dresses, came to dinner one night and everyone dined on the patio. The Americans showed little interest in me.

When they were gone the poet said: 'Tomorrow you'll be gone and nothing I say will make any difference.'

On the wall there was a signed black-and-white photograph of Anna Akhmatova. He'd met her in Taormina in 1964 when she'd been awarded the Taormina Prize.

Before I left he gave me a book of her poems. I saw dolphins in the Aegean on my way back to the mainland.

In a café in Belgrade there was a bunch of marigolds beside a bottle of white wine in half-wicker.

Rena's voice returned with some information the old nun had given her.

'Emile Gravelet, "Blondin", stood upon his head, wheeled a man in a barrow blindfold and cooked an omelette on a stove on a tightrope across the Niagara Falls.'

A raven had lived near the convent and once stole one of the nuns' habits for its nest.

Did I know what ravens' eggs looked like, Rena asked me on a boat in San Francisco Bay.

Remarkably small for the size of the bird, pale blue or pale green, dark-brown spots and ashy markings, but sometimes just pale blue.

It's like painting a bunch of marigolds, I thought, years later in southern California, to keep the light, to make something. It's to accept the gravity of the marigolds; marigolds on the station platform of a small town in County Galway; a bunch of marigolds on a shelf in a café in Belgrade on a Fall morning.

There are frontiers beyond which a person can't go, frontiers of shatterment. My friend vanished into a village of condominiums and caravans in northern California. Often in the British Library in London, placed in a book, I'd come across a card for the religious group she'd joined, an emblem of laminated pink rosebuds on what could have been the silver of an old man's hair.

Little Friends

Recently I came across a red Silvine exercise book with a sentence of Eugène Delacroix's I jotted down when I was sixteen: 'To finish demands a heart of steel ...'

He has gone to the place
Where naught can delight him.
He may sit now and tell of the sights he has seen of,
While forlorn he does mourn on the Isle of St Helena.

Ailve Ó Cóileáin came from a place not far from where Daniel O'Connell, the Liberator, was born, where leviathans could regularly be sighted.

In the late-eighteenth century his family defied the Penal Laws, sending their children to school in France, building handsome houses from lime and cows' blood, storing the beeves in autumn for winter and feasting far from London, from the nucleus of an Empire that had hastily broken the terms of the Treaty of Limerick and, in response to the War of the Spanish Succession, which brought the aged Louis XIV to the gates of Amsterdam, intensified the Penal Laws.

Priests in the instinct-red vestments of the eighteenth century had continued to say Mass through the Penal Laws here where the common puffin, the red puffin, the seal lived and iodine was exported from here to Seville where Murillo had painted the pelota players and the water-sellers when his wife died after twenty years of marriage.

Ailve's family owned a Swiss castle-hotel with a bar to the side with an advertisement outside for Turf Virginia Cigarettes with a picture of a centaur on the packet.

Two of the customers in blue serge suits sent from the United States would join their foreheads as they sang a song together about Napoleon.

Framed in the bar was a cartoon from the *Empire News* of a local butcher-businessman from whom Buckingham Palace had ordered pork just after the Second World War and who had the pigs killed on the mail boat in the middle of the Irish Sea so they'd be fresh for the royal feast.

St Gobnait, patron saint of bees, and in County Kerry usurping St Brigid as patron saint of blacksmiths, had lived near here. She had the power to carry live coals in her apron. Once she went to the forge for coals. Idlers were hanging around the forge. She put the coals in her apron, lifting her skirts to miniskirt level. 'Nice pair of legs,' a lecher declared. She was thrilled with the compliment and immediately the coals burned through her apron and she lost the power forever.

Starlings came from all over the British Isles here for the winter and had rallies. They were great mimickers and could mimic the lamentation of the herring gull.

'I'm an autumn person,' Ailve told me, over a mug with a ladybird – *une coccinelle* – on it, at the first French lesson.

Eyebright, with its lonely flame, grew on the cliffs in August.

Burnet moths, olive wings stippled with scarlet, on the cliff scabious in September.

The tree mallow still flourishing in October, where the butcher-businessman dispatched pigeons with gold to England after the Second World War when gold was scarce there.

The fly agaric mushroom, blood-luminous and yellow, in November, where the storyteller Seán Ó Conaill went from house to house.

In December necklaces of birds' footprints on the beaches, the cries of the winter birds like the full-time whistle at a Gaelic football match, tortoiseshell sunshine.

Ailve had a host of relatives who were nuns in France and at fifteen she was sent to a convent in Paris, where at the end of the war, thanks to the Irish Red Cross, which included some of Ailve's relatives, Tipperary cheese in a box with a picture of a cow on it had been in vogue.

Leaving Ireland she had to say goodbye to a Gaelic student who saved the hay with farmers where the kings of Kerry used to booley — leave their permanent residence and graze their cattle for the summer.

But she had a Kodak colour photograph with a white border, a boy with cranberry-auburn hair.

At school in Kerry she'd been taught the eighteenth-century Killarney poet, Aogán Ó Rathaille, who lamented he'd got no periwinkles as a child. He wrote of visions, the Beautiful Lady. Ailve found the Beautiful Lady again in a Russian church in Paris – Holy Sophia.

After a few years she attended the Sorbonne.

Her beloved Proust saw Queen Alexandra with followers approach a Parisian buffet table in royal procession.

Ailve saw the Duke of Windsor in linen jacket and white buckskin shoes in the Bois de Boulogne.

I learnt from her at the first French lesson that Racine had written about the Duke and Duchess of Windsor situation centuries before in *Bérénice*.

I was sixteen when I met Ailve, autumn 1967.

She was teaching French for a year in a convent with a statue of St Rose of Lima, first saint of the Americas, outside it, in the town where I lived.

I started going to her for French lessons, bringing red Silvine exercise books.

'My little friends,' she told me Gauguin called the postcards on his wall and her postcards, in a room overlooking the river, were Proust's friend Robert de Montesquiou in Napoleonic-green coat by Lucien Doucet; Berthe Morisot's portrait of her sister in ultramarine dog collar and mother in black Second Empire gown; *Salome* by Delacroix; *Lot's Wife Turning to Salt* by Maître François.

A few years before my father had bought me a set of art books. Loose colour reproductions went with them and one of them had been Dürer's *Lot and his Daughters*: a loftily turbaned Lot leaving Sodom with wine slung over his shoulder, which he's later to drink and lie down with his daughters and have children by them; basket of eggs in hand; one daughter merrily with the family moneybox although her mother has visibly turned into a pillar of salt behind her. When Sodom was burned, Proust noted that a few of those sodomites had managed to escape, Ailve illuminated me.

She would play arias from *Iphigénie en Aulide*, which Pauline Viardot used to sing to Flaubert in his Turkish knitted waistcoat with brown-and-red stripes and green oriental slippers.

Pride of place on her shelf was the Penguin Classic edition of Flaubert's *Bouvard and Pécuchet* with *The Farmers of Flagey* returning from the fair by Courbet on the cover, and she called the fair that had just ended in the town a 'pardon'.

Many Travellers stayed in the countryside near the town for the winter after the fair.

The Traveller children could indicate the hazelnut and the wild plum for you. The heron was anthropoid for them, and the ferret.

What really brought Ailve here I never knew.

Her elfin face was distinctive above a black polo-neck sweater, her legs in lurex-thread stretch tights or ribbed orange tights under a mid-thigh miniskirt, her hair, brown-blonde, a little bucket of it, nearly unkempt, not quite, her eyes the green of the dado on the stairway. But it was her clown's mouth, her Toulouse-Lautrec Cirque Fernando mouth, that distinguished her most of all.

She told me about Paris: blue scooters, Brigitte Bardot ponytails, ankle-length ladies' pants, zip-fastened jackets, ski socks, scarlet armlets on First Holy Communicants, Chanel lipstick.

Her own lipstick was usually tiger-lily red.

In Paris she never stopped thinking of Daniel O'Connell, who witnessed the bloodbath of the Revolution and henceforth vowed himself to peaceful means, dying of heartbreak in Genoa, May 1847, on his way to Rome to pray for famine-stricken Ireland.

Bonfires had lit all over Ailve's peninsula in 1829 for Catholic Emancipation as bonfires were still lit in east Galway near Offaly, on

Midsummer's Night, groups of young men, shirts off, holding hands, jumping over them in unison to airs on a squeezebox like 'Seán South of Garryowen'.

'For he fell beneath a Northern sky, brave Hanlon at his side.'

After two lessons Ailve told me about her affair with an Austrian novelist called David. He was inquisitive about her because so many of the Wild Geese – Irish soldiers who'd fled the Jacobite Wars – had gone to Austria.

Maria Theresa, who had Goldkette the rope dancer and bareback rider perform at her coronation ceremony and had emancipated Gypsies, appointed Count Browne of Limerick as commander-in-chief of her armies.

Ailve had a Polaroid photograph of David, taken at a terrace café in Italian sunglasses, jacket with a Persian-lamb collar.

She was adamant that theirs had not been primarily a sexual relationship but spiritual, an elevating of things into a vision.

Mutually looking at Rodin's sculpture *La Pensée* – a woman's head in deep thought – Ailve had been struck by its totality, the way it expressed the coming together of things, adolescence and adulthood, a moment when one was self-aware and self-welcoming.

Ailve and David touched, they briefed one another in their individual pain but he faded into the romanticism of other flesh – male as well as female.

She finished at the Sorbonne, returned to Kerry, but not before, like St Gobnait, she showed her legs, making love to American GIs with skin felted like the wild raspberry, hair blonde as canary grass, who had the mock orange of Idaho or the flowering dogwood of North Carolina embroidered on their uniforms; Japanese tourists who wore Jean-Paul Sartre jackets; not to mention wealthy Parisian bachelors who wore glove-fitting jeans, in apartments on the boulevard des Italiens, avenue de l'Opéra, boulevard Montmartre.

Ailve and I had tea and tipsy cake – pink icing, sponge base with chocolate fondant, jam syrup and sherry.

'Oh God,' she cried. 'Where are they? The painters, the writers, the musicians, more than anything the young, the young in spirit?'

She began having an affair with Jerome Denmyr, an engineer with collar-length hair, who was from a town where an Irish revolutionary's handcuffs were kissed by his mother as he was taken away in 1918. On Sundays she went to the mental-hospital grounds to see him play rugby. Mental-hospital patients stared from behind iron bars. The heron was the totem of this town and there was always one making a journey along the nearby river. After the rugby matches Jerome always smelled of American Bay Rum.

People stood around the gallery during dances in the local ballroom they went to together – the artistes were Maisie McDaniels in bootlace tie, miniskirt, Edwardian pantomime-boy boots; Butch Moore with silver-dollar crew cut and polo-neck shirt; Joe Dolan in mauve jacket; Eileen Reid in air-hostess's outfit; Dickie Rock and the Miami Showband in plum-coloured blazers and trousers with knife-sharp creases – various laps to the evening until eventually lights lowered, red, girls' arms intricated around men's shoulders.

Alternatively they went in his Volkswagen Beetle to the Prince of Wales Hotel in Athlone, which I always imagined to be called after the Duke of Windsor, who, in his pancake cap and smoking a shag cigarette, on a visit to the United States in 1922, when asked by a hostess who he wanted on the guest list, picked the Dolly Sisters as his first choice, which gave enormous joy to the gossip columnist Cholly Knickerbocker.

Ailve wore a black silk brocade dress when she was with him, a cotton Watteau dairymaid dress, or a dress with multi-coloured paisley design.

Balzac, she said by way of explanation, had one of his heroines wear a different dress for every meeting with her lover.

On a sojourn back in Paris from Tahiti, on his walks home with his adolescent girlfriend Judith Molard, Gauguin nightly pissed in the courtyard.

Jerome would piss in the courtyard of Ailve's house at night on his way back from the pub with her.

Judith Molard bought flowers for Gauguin when he was leaving for Tahiti for the last time, but because the colours were too nondescript for one who was lavish with Veronese greens, she was ashamed and threw them away.

'And where are the flowers here, might I ask?' Ailve deplored.

She often quoted Maude Gonne McBride in old age when she

was photographed by Horvath with a lioness-face brooch at her throat: 'My heart is for Ireland and my love for France.'

The floods grew higher and she was like one of those mental-hospital patients behind iron bars. Her face became thin and papier-mâché-like. Her eyes grew large, looming even, and her mouth grew longer, more tragic, an entrée clown's mouth.

I wanted to believe everything she told me about her life. Sometimes I doubted. But what one could not easily dispense with was an image, an inspiration, Rodin's *La Pensée* – 'The Thought' – self-confrontation, the tentative approach to a work of art that for one moment objectifies our life, arrests its flow, creating something, wonder in the eyes, remorse in the heart, sublimation.

Ailve saw herself through that sculpture, a girl in Paris, in a short, black, plastic wrapover coat, and scarf with large geometric patterns.

Her stories about French literature became more prolific.

How Flaubert was inspired to write *Madame Bovary* by a woman's face he saw as a young man in a small town in Brittany. Her Penguin Classic edition featured *Madame de Calonne* by Gustave Ricard on the cover.

How George Sands used to jump into icy water to cure herself of illness. How one of the duchesses Proust wrote about died of starvation during the Occupation and was eaten by one of her own greyhounds.

And she might end with one about Vincent Van Gogh: how he had a print – a little friend – of Irish emigrants on his wall.

When I mentioned after Christmas I'd seen the pantomime *Cinderella* in Dublin she retold Charles Perrault's *Cinderella* as Seán Ó Conaill might tell a story; the pumpkin turned into a gilded coach; the mice turned into mouse-coloured horses; the rat turned into a coachman; the lizards turned into footmen.

When I was a child the mother in a family farther up the street had been from Warsaw where her house had been lit by gas lamps in childhood.

They had a book with an illustration of Charlotte, one of the ugly sisters, in an ultramarine-ash wig and ice-green ruffles.

They also had a book with illustrations of a fox in scarlet hunting jacket and a woman in a coal-skuttle hat, with peach cape, riding a goose.

I asked the Little Lord Fauntleroy son if he'd be my friend but he categorically said, 'No.'

I felt like Cinderella when addressed by Charlotte as 'Cinderbreech'.

Through Ailve's affair with Jerome Denmyr she was a daily Communicant at Mass, going to the altar in a Cossack hat, a straw boater with Hawaiian ribbon-band, or beret with brooch trim.

Spring came with bird-cherry blossom on the outskirts of town.

Ailve wrote a letter to Mr Brezhnev about women political prisoners in the small zone unit at Barashevo in Mordovia.

Solzhenitsyn got eight years, she reminded me, for referring to Stalin as 'the whiskered one'. 'Be careful what you say.'

She accompanied me to François Truffaut's *Fahrenheit 451* in the town hall.

I wore a cravat patterned with orange-coloured prints of a potato-cut done in art class. She wore a suit with polka-dotted Peter Pan collar and decorative polka-dotted handkerchief in breast pocket.

Literature is banned. Men in boiler suits seize books. Mechanical hounds with needles shoot transgressors. Helicopters drop bombs. People retire to the mountains, light fires, and, to keep them alive, recite aloud, individual people with the task of an individual author, *Wuthering Heights* by Emily Brontë, the stories of Matthew, Mark, Luke and John.

'As soon as they were come to land, they saw a fire of coals there ...'

Ailve returned from a weekend in Kerry, where she'd gone to a country-and-western night at the Gleneagle Hotel, Killarney, and told me she was pregnant.

What would she do?

Have an abortion, she decided. Like any good Catholic Irish teacher.

I was due to go to France on a student-exchange scheme but I volunteered to run away and join her in London.

No, she said, Jerome was going with her.

'No use dragging you into it.'

She was wearing flared pants with spotted hyenas on them and large hoop earrings.

'I came back to be mediocre again, to re-establish that part of myself. Now look at me. Having an abortion with a man who sweats too much.'

I was moved by her and without warning she was in my arms, weeping, feeling the width and breadth of my shoulders as I conquered her waist, a little package in a blouse as white as an Arlésienne's Holy Communion dress.

'Do not forget to go to see Rodin's *La Pensée*,' she told me, as if making her last will and testament.

She gave me a gift of a bloater tie intended for Jerome, with a pattern of Camberwell butterflies, deep yellow with purple borders, telling me how Princess Mathilde, Napoleon's niece, gave Proust some silk from one of her dresses to make a cravat.

The sycamore blossomed and the oak, the chestnut trees that could have been planted, like Stendhal's in the days of the Sforzas, when, in a blue-and-white fleck suit, Miss Ó Cóileáin drove away in a cherry-red Renault, after a gala day in the convent – when an extract from Racine's *Bérénice* was enacted as it first had been by the young ladies of Madame de Maintenon's Academy attached to the court of Louis XIV – skedaddling off to Kerry, thence to London.

'A sad example of the Sleights of Love.'

For the performance I had worn a Sergeant Pepper shirt patterned with black-eyed Susans my mother had bought for me in Dublin.

Ailve wrote to me in Paris that summer.

> *16 Bolingbroke Road,*
> *London W14,*
> *23 August 1968*

Desmond, a Chara,
It is the Feast of St Rose of Lima.

    Had my abortion. It was like a butterfly slipping away.

    I went to the Church of the Benedictine Adorers of the Sacred Heart of Montmartre in Marble Arch afterwards.

    It's very hot here, scorching. The dustbins are overflowing. Stendhal said the soul goes down in price in England.

    Jerome plays Radio Luxembourg late into the night.

I put a PG tips historical card of Mary Stuart, one-time Queen of France, on the mantlepiece.

Ronsard said her fingers were like the branch of a tree. He also wrote a poem about her opponent, Elizabeth I, who sent him a gold sovereign for his efforts.

I'm alone here, thinking of a Kerryman who was educated in France.

'The freedom of Ireland is not worth the shedding of a single drop of blood.'

I feel I've killed something for Ireland, the baby within me. There's a space within me they can't fill, the nuns, the schoolgirls, the statues of St Rose of Lima.

It will go on and on, gathering force like a huge wave. I wish you were here. I know you'd understand but even you couldn't stop it.

I've murdered a part of myself and buried it under the floor of a classroom.

Lots of kisses,

Ailve

On Ailve's recommendation I went to see Édouard Manet's portrait of his sister-in-law Berthe Morisot in the Musée d'Orsay but was dismayed to find the entire face was covered with a fan.

I also went to see Rodin's *La Pensée*.

In a wet and grey summer, staying in a suburb, nearby factories emitting flames that burned into the mind, it was the highlight, this wonder of marble.

Looking at it I confronted a fragment of myself, a boy in a white shirt with a peaked collar who had complimented a girl in a white blouse.

I wondered if it had been real, her affair in Paris, but knew that it didn't matter because we'd been real, we'd touched, my head had sunk into hers and our mutual tremor would shake our lives, going on and on when guns raged in another part of Ireland.

When I returned to Ireland that autumn she was nowhere to be seen. Jerome Denmyr was back, excelling himself on the rugby pitch.

In Buenos Aires Manchester United's Nobby Stiles was back-headed in the face by an Estudiantes player, and El Beatle, George Best, at the height of his pudding-bowl pompadour, took appropriate reprisals.

Peter Sarstedt sang 'Where Do You Go To (My Lovely)?' from Enzo's Café.

I wondered what had happened to her. Had she died from the after-effects of abortion?

Had she returned to Paris as she said she might?

In either case I was determined on going on, the shadow of a Rodin sculpture inside, the knowledge gained from art that life is worth holding on to, that if you keep fighting it will come, freedom.

Ailve had given me the first lesson in freedom.

It was up to me to go on, rung by rung, until I met someone or something that touched me again as deeply as Rodin's *La Pensée*.

I travelled. I saw the pearwood Virgin in Chartres Cathedral, the statuette of Philosophus outside it again; I visited Stes-Maries-de-la-Mer, to which the black Madonna was borne on a cloud of red sand, in a house or stone coffin, with the other two Maries. I saw a Spanish Mercheros Gypsies' encampment, just like a painting by Van Gogh, by a necropolis and young blonde German Jenisch Gypsies in wingtip shoes in cafés where the jukeboxes played *Schlagermusik* sung by Czech Vlachs Gypsies.

My little friends were Gauguin's naked *Breton Boy*, strong black lines separating his body from the grass he's lying on; Van Gogh's night-time café in Arles, which he painted with candles in his hat; Vermeer's *View of Delft*.

Ailve had told me the story.

Proust thought *View of Delft*, which he saw as a young man, the most beautiful painting in the world. A few years before he died there was a Vermeer exhibition at the Jeu de Paume. He temporarily collapsed before going to it. There he saw *View of Delft* again and still thought it the most beautiful painting in the world.

Another of her stories had been about the Liberator's poetess aunt Eibhlín Dhubh Ní Chonaill who married Art Ó Laoghaire, a young captain in the Hungarian Hussars and lived with him near Macroom, west Cork.

Art had a bitter quarrel with Abraham Morris, the high sheriff, and was shot dead by Morris's bodyguard.

When Art's sister arrived from Cork city for the wake she was outraged to find Eibhlín in bed, that she wasn't mourning sufficiently.

The accusation of not mourning enough was always being flung at me.

It was flung once more at me when most of the members of the Miami Showband, which Ailve regularly danced to, were murdered on their way back from a country-and-western night near Newry, County Down.

When Sandy Denny — wind-blown blonde hair, sunburst jellabas — who sang songs as old as Chaucer's 'Poor Person' or Blind Mary's father John Bunyan, died as a result of falling down a stairs, I heard that Ailve, after a brief career as an actress in Dublin, had married a politician.

In her brief career as an actress in a cul-de-sac theatre, she'd played Beatrice in Stendhal's play *The Cenci*, about an Italian count who raped his daughter; she in turn tortured and murdered for her part in his murder. It was in this role, for which she won considerable acclaim, that Ailve caught the politician's attention.

Some years later I visited her in Galway.

A pathway led to a white house that was identical to the illimitable miles of white houses that swept around me.

In an exercise suit patterned with palm leaves, blue canvas beach shoes, hair with long fringe now, Ailve answered the door, half-fearfully, her face sunken in.

When Queen Elizabeth, who receives a sprig of thorn each Easter from Glastonbury where the Irish monks used to venerate Patrick, visited the dying Duke of Windsor in Paris, and there was a Georges de la Tour exhibition in the Orangerie des Tuileries, which did for de la Tour, not overlooked by Ailve's Proust, what an exhibition in Milan in 1951 did for Caravaggio, she had returned to Paris as she suggested she might but found the streets forever led back to a street in Kerry where there were Holy Communion dresses in full blossom in one shop window, which always had messages about lost keys.

When you see life through a maze of fifteen thousand novels, you must get a queer impression of things and see them from an odd angle, Flaubert's cousin Guy de Maupassant said.

The fifteen thousand novels had led us both to fifteen thousand suburban houses.

Ailve showed me in.

Black flags had been flying in County Mayo, which I'd just returned from, for the recent H-Block deaths, as they'd flown throughout Ireland early in 1957 for Seán South from Henry Street, Limerick, and Feargal O'Hanlon from Monaghan town, killed during an attack on a police barracks in County Fermanagh, and the country-and-western voice of Louise Corrigan, from Bansha, County Tipperary, where a girl was tortured to death as a witch at the end of the nineteenth century, sounded from every café.

On Ailve's Laura Ashley wallpaper was a reproduction of the Belfast artist Paul Henry's painting of the two Umhall mountains in County Mayo, with Knockmore on Clare Island to the west.

When the French landed in Killala in County Mayo in 1798, a County Mayo landlord's son was declared president of the republic of Connaught.

On a beanbag cushion was a book, *Cinderella*, a palace garden with trees in blossom on the cover.

Ailve's children were Segda, a girl, and Breffni, a boy.

My first impulse was to embrace her but I was restrained by the look on her face.

Ailve Ó Cóileáin looked at me and I saw myself, for the first time in years — rooms full of little friends, and suddenly as if the little friends went up in flames, having to move on — still trying as she tried, her face white and sunken now but her eyes still burning and alive, repeating themselves over and over in my mind just as the white houses of the republic of Connaught repeated themselves, over and over again, until they reached the sea.

Shelter

They're seasonal. Like the laughing goose.

They come to the art-deco shelter on Sunday evenings in January.

Boys from Greenmount in the south of Cork city in Manchester United bobble hats, baseball caps with slogans like 'Whip Me' or 'Yankees', Crusaders' headdresses from Dunnes Stores, cowls. Many of them with blotched faces like the spots on the woundwort flower.

They're typical of groups of boys you see in Cork or Limerick, who have no association with female company, and who are obsessed with soccer.

In January they have neophytes, sixteen-year-old boys, down over their lips like the teeth of the dog's-tooth violet, with faces like kittiwakes or guillemots and Damien Duff razor shaves, sea-anemone ear studs or maybe white plastic rosaries or pendants with gold knobs of Our Lord's head around their necks under a Cristiano Ronaldo T-shirt or T-shirt with a 2Pac epitaph: 'Only God can judge me!'

In Greenmount in Cork they have sex games with one another in a shed.

But more often than not they play shadow games – they mime what each other is doing.

Or they might retell a legend learned at community college, like how Fionn MacChumhaill was the Hercules of Ireland and another

Hercules, Cúchulainn — no one knew whether he was Scottish or Irish, Celtic or Rangers — came to fight with him.

Fionn MacChumhaill lay in a cradle, pretending he was a baby, bit off the middle finger of Cúchulainn's right hand — his strength — and then killed him.

In the shed is a poster of Mayfield's Roy Keane, of Cúchulainn-stature, in an Etruscan-red jersey, black knee-high stockings with scarlet tops, which have galloons of gold, beside a picture of Princess Diana in cream linen jeans holding a child in Bosnia; David Beckham with a topknot; Wayne Rooney just out of De La Salle in Croxteth kicking a ball; Keanu Reeves in a shirt of gold brocade patterned with blue-and-red blossom and green foliage, and codpiece, as Don John in *Much Ado About Nothing*.

'I had rather be a canker in a hedge than a rose in his grace.'

In the summer in cobweb-muscle T-shirts they pick potatoes near Bandon, which was settled with Somerset people in Shakespeare's day.

On summer evenings, in the hoops — emerald and white of Celtic — they congregate at the mallard sanctuary in the Lee Fields where elderly men lie way out on the Lee as if it was a jacuzzi.

On Saturdays they watch soccer at Turner's Cross, originally home of Evergreen United.

In the 1950s soccer was played at the Mardyke, home of Cork Athletic.

There were no toilet facilities at the Mardyke in the 1950s and men and boys urinated over the stiles. Soccer was a phallic tradition in Cork.

Black and Tans, called after a pack of hounds in south Tipperary, once played soccer on the greenswards of Cork in zebra-striped jerseys, jerseys with enlarged vertical stripes of black and white. Some of them did charity work with a boys' club in Greenmount.

Others of their number, using trench ladders, during a Gaelic football match in November 1920, stormed Croke Park and shot dead thirteen people, including three boys of ten, eleven, fourteen, and the Grangemockler cornerback Michael Hogan in white-and-gold Tipperary stripe.

Poinsettia red is the colour of the Cork Gaelic team and in

O'Keefe Park in Black-and-Tan days it was customary to start matches with the singing, by a soloist in a bowler hat with a red carnation in his lapel, of 'My Dark Rosaleen':

> O my Dark Rosaleen
> Do not sigh, do not weep!
> The priests are on the ocean green,
> They march along the deep.
> There's wine from the royal Pope
> Upon the ocean green ...

The Palace Theatre of Varieties opened in King Street, Cork, Easter 1897, with the overture to *Semiramide*, by Rossini, the Miller Girls in Gainsborough costumes singing 'By Shannon's Dancing Waters', the good fairy Goldenstar doing a leg-show in front of a backdrop of Pope's Quay, and it didn't close before Fred Karno brought his Ladies' Soccer Team in blue-and-white Kilmarnock stripe.

'My Old man is one of the Boys and I am one of the Girls.'

Speedwell is one of the first flowers to come to the coast and one of the last to leave. Crimthann's eyes are speedwell blue. He is relatively small, like Tottenham Spurs' Robbie Keane. Hair cut Turkish style – slash at the side, slash in the brow.

The barber in Cork who cut his hair has a statuette in his shop of a clown-client in a barber's chair seizing the clippers from a bobby barber.

On a January Sunday evening, the pharos on Loop Head in County Clare signalling, Crimthann sits alone in the shelter.

His father buys antiques – a painting of Judith with the head of Holofernes, a statuette of Charlie Chaplin in pumps with white laces seated under a lamppost with a dog – and sells them.

'My grandparents are Pavvies in Kilmallock. My parents are Buffers in Greenmount. My cousins are Rathkealers.'

In the front garden of his Greenmount home is a nymph with outsized breasts on a petalled stone mound, two cherubs who look as if they'd done military service with the task of holding up the urn.

Many of the Buffer – settled – Traveller boys in Greenmount now play soccer whereas they once played hurling and Gaelic foot-ball. Their soccer team recently won against the guards' team. There used to be a notorious remand home in Greenmount near St Finbarr's Cathedral.

But the worst fate was to be sent to one in Dangan, County Offaly, in the midlands.

Some of Crimthann's group ventured to work in the meat factory in Charleville, in north-west Cork, where there were fights with slash hooks and pickaxe handles on Saturday nights. A few went to work in Pat Grace's Famous Fried Chicken in Dublin – Pat Grace had managed the Limerick soccer team for a while. Others went to Germany where they invested their earnings twice a month in the Deutsche Bundesbank.

But when Steven Gerrard made his debut playing against Ukraine, Crimthann went to England.

David Beckham and Posh Spice being married, on the wall of a room in Dollis Hill, in angel-white Confederate tails and oyster satin antebellum dress, by the Protestant Bishop of Cork, in Luttrellstown Castle, County Dublin, which the Bishop blessed so the marriage could take place in it; David Beckham and Posh Spice in identical mulberry change of gear, cutting the cake, which looked, taking its theme from the castle grounds, as if it was adorned with marzipan honeysuckle and marzipan holly.

For the first few weeks Crimthann worked laying pipes for McNicholls in Thornton Heath. Originally two brothers from Bahoula, County Mayo – one brother with green trucks, the other brother with brown trucks.

He took a ride on a black Shetland pony on Weymouth Strand, sprouted with Union Jack sunscreens; sat under a London pub mirror decorated with eagles, phoenixes, sheaves of wheat in warm gold and cold silver, for a striptease to an Eminem song by a boy in an American football helmet, fishnet football jersey, jocks; swam in Blackpool in October where a member of the Manchester United Youth Team had once famously walked out of a guesthouse in hiwaist swimming togs to avoid paying his bill to a Jayne Mansfield lookalike landlady and changed into bumfreezer jacket and tie with small knot and square ends, on the Golden Mile.

Union Jack bunting on the Golden Mile; women with dicky-bow earrings or fake-pearl ties linking arms with Morecambe-and-Wise husbands; illuminations of the tower, of a ferris wheel, of the dodgems reflected in the Irish Sea.

Crimthann's grandfather, who had a greyhound called Dinny and a shihtzu called Sheila, had once taken a cattle boat from Cobh and seen a flea circus in Blackpool and Dick Turpin's ride to York re-enacted in a circus.

Wall's ice cream; Brylcreem; Durex — 'Better for Both'; Movietone News; fish and chips on Friday nights; black shirts with white buttons.

Thick cotton soccer jerseys with stiff collars and billowing shorts — but Duncan Edwards, the Greek *kouros*, defied them by rolling the elastic on his waist to show his thighs.

Duncan Edwards' face in an Oxford frame — Cinestar quiff, laconic smile — a Greenmount family legend; Munich …

Crimthann's grandfather told him how, just after the Second World War, Moscow Dynamos, in blue, presented their opponents, Chelsea, in red then, not the gentian blue of now, with bunches of red carnations before a game at Stamford Bridge.

Ten years later, the Roman Catholic Church banned attendance at a match in Dalymount Park, Dublin, between Ireland and Yugoslavia, because Yugoslavia was a communist country, but 33,000 people turned up.

'My grandfather in the Seychelles cussed me for being light-skinned,' an elderly black woman in a coat fastened with loops and bone toggles, in the Royal Take Away on the South Pier, said to him.

'He was a communist. Nearly threw myself under a bus when he died. My dad went to America then. My mother left for England with me and my sister. We lived in Sunderland on the Wear, between the Tyne and the Tees, at first.

'It was just after the war. When the lights went on again, all over the world.

'My mother died. Then we moved to Blackpool. My sister was always telling me what to do. And I said, it's like locking the gate on an ass that's galloping in the fields.

'Met a boy on the Golden Mile. His name was Marshall. Marshall Gold. A coincidence. He had apple-blossom waves of hair. Parma violets in his lapel.

' "How does it feel to be handsome?" I said. "Is it alright?"

' "You've a nice body," he said. "It's your face that's the problem. I'm in the travel business," he said. "I take trips to Jamaica. Will you travel with me?"

'Went out with him for a few years. Watched Alf Ramsey and Stan Matthews play at Bloomfield Road with him.

'Walked with him by the lights of the Festival of Britain in London.

'The rock-and-roll cafés were springing up nineteen to a dozen in Blackpool.

'I cut my wrists. I was in love and all that. But the dead dwell in a land of no return.

'Where there's life there's hope. Now I'm satisfied with my life. Just as it is. I'm getting older bit by bit, day by day, and I don't notice. Lord have mercy.'

Crimthann knew of Salome's dance, but now there were male Salomes.

Boys in London pubs who dropped quilted workman's trousers to reveal Calvin Klein, Armani, Lonsdale, aussieBum underwear, and then dropped their underwear. Boys naked but for jungle-army fatigue caps held at their crotch. Apricot-coloured boiler-suit acts.

But the most popular were soccer and rugger acts. The difference was that the Will Carling or Daragh O'Shea lookalike rugger boys held balls for their acts.

A rugger stripper might be marigold hirsute; a soccer stripper a beetroot-coloured adolescent boy's penis.

At one of these shows the boy beside him, with shot-gold brindled hair, shot-gold goat's beard, told him the story of the Jacobean-featured David Scarboro who once played Mark Fowler, a confused teenager in *EastEnders* on television.

He felt trapped, typecast, and left the programme.

Even if he tried for ordinary jobs he was seen as Mark Fowler.

He became clinically depressed and was admitted to a mental hospital.

On his return home telephoto lenses were focussed on his bedroom by England's paparazzi.

The paparazzi claimed he was known in his village as Dracula because he was white as a sheet and emerged from his home only at night.

He became overwhelmed by this persecution and his body was found at the bottom of Beachy Head, near Eastbourne, East Sussex.

> Are you going to Scarborough Fair?
> Parsley, sage, rosemary and thyme,
> Remember me to one who lives there,
> For he once was a true love of mine.

> Did ye ever travel twixt Berwick and Lyne?
> Sober and grave grows merry in time
> There ye'll meet wi' a handsome young man
> Ance he was a true love o' mine.

Crimthann would trek Hampstead Heath late afternoons. The houses on the margin of the Heath lighted up. Wine doors, diamond-glass windows, floriated lace curtains, lozenge shapes in the transoms, Japanese red maple trees in the cobbled front yards, rock-rose bushes.

Other people's homes.

The crested grebe with their black-and-grey summer head-dresses live on Hampstead Heath. Flocks of seven or eight pass over the Heath, diving into Highgate ponds, making sounds like a hawk swooping for prey. Frequently, crested grebe are drowned by fishermen's nets in the ponds, as are cygnets.

The coots build their nests in the lifebuoys on the ponds with stalk, leaves of bulrushes, flag, reed, mace reed.

Like the crested grebe they cover their eggs with weeds.

The continental fighting coot comes in winter to the Heath, passing over Beachy Head on the way, and when the ponds are frozen fight other birds on the ice, with their feet as well as their beaks.

'We sailed by Beachy, by Fairlight and Dover.'

In a dingle on the Heath a man with a walrus moustache, chinless face, tattoo of a woman in bondage gear on his belly, who said he was from Chingford, Essex, enticed Crimthann to use poppers.

He tried to force Crimthann to have sex with him.

'You've done the Paddy on me,' he shouted after Crimthann as Crimthann walked away.

In the all-night café at Victoria Station, fake rose in a Panda orangeade tin, Crimthann had tea in a mug with Princess Diana on it in a poppy dress, with a boy with filamented hair, mushroom ears and explosions of green eyes, who said he was a boxer.

'I've lived in Liverpool, Ringsend and Galway. I was a heavy-weight. Now I'm a middleweight.'

Crimthann remembered a story from community college, where they were continually reminded that in Iraq soccer players who played badly were tortured; how in early May 1916, Countess Markievicz, who'd worn a slouch hat with cock feathers and a green tunic with silver buttons for the Rising, sentenced to death, each morning hearing the shots as her comrades were executed, heard a tap on the prison door.

The teenage British soldier with Mancunian accent, standing guard outside, unlocked the door, let himself in, offered her a shag cigarette and talked with her through the night.

He'd seen Liverpool play Burnley at Crystal Palace when King George V, who bathed the golden-haired, pink-skinned Prince Edward himself while Queen Mary looked on in a choker of uncut emeralds, was present.

He produced a cigarette-box picture from his pocket of Adonis-faced Steve Bloomer, then interned in Ruhleben in Germany, who'd played for Derby, in quartered cap, against a balustrade trussed with tea roses.

The reprieved Countess Markievicz was haunted by this young soccer fan for the rest of her life and thought to go searching for him, a face, but decided she might get him into trouble if she revealed what he'd done.

'I live in King's Cross,' the boxer said, 'dreadful place. Six-year-olds beat up a woman in a wheelchair.'

Jack Doyle, the boxer, a stevedore from Cobh, County Cork, home of the Cobh Ramblers, had drawn an audience of 90,000 in White City in the 1930s, starred in two films, married a Mexican film star, Movita, with Remembrance Day-red lips.

Toured England with her as a double singing act. Remarried her to national headlines in St Andrew's Church, Westland Row, Dublin.

She left him to wed Marlon Brando. Later in life Jack Doyle

became a tramp with a red carnation in his buttonhole.

Crimthann's last days in England were spent sleeping in a shop-front near Victoria Station until 9.30, spending the day in the day centre in Carlisle Street, intermittently going to admire the portrait of Queen Sophia Charlotte, who wore a high white wig, in an outspread gown studded with little bows, in the Queen's Gallery where the attendant, who wore a waistcoat with gold threaded stripes, coarse velvet knee breeches, buckled pumps, was from Crumlin, Dublin – terraced or semi-detached 1930s house – where Niall Quinn was from.

Crimthann had been good at art at community college, which was taught through Gaelic.

There'd been a teacher at community college with a grin like a Cheshire cat who invited some of the boys home and showed them penitentiary pornographic films or naked soccer matches on Copacabana and Ipanema beaches in Brazil.

When Crimthann had been at community college, Ed O'Brien, a young IRA volunteer from the Irish Republic, accidentally blew himself up aboard a London double-decker bus while ferrying a bomb to its intended target, injuring several passengers.

Grief-stricken and deeply shamed parents greeted his body as it crossed into the Irish Republic.

In January 1957, 20,000 people had turned out in Limerick for the funeral of Seán South, a clerk at a Limerick timber firm and founder of a Limerick branch of Maria Duce, a right-wing Roman Catholic association, who was killed during an attack on Brookeborough RUC Barracks in County Fermanagh, including Crimthann's family, the Brogans, who watched it from the O'Connell Monument.

Men with black armlets and men in the olive-green Fianna Éireann uniforms flanked the motor hearse, which had difficulty passing through the streets, the crowds were so dense.

Lord mayors, county and urban councillors, city corporation members, Roman Catholic dignitaries, had all extended their sympathy to Seán South's widowed mother and his two brothers.

In Greenmount in Cork, beside a photograph of Duncan Edwards, was a photograph of Seán South – Maureen O'Hara-red hair, wire glasses like Pope Pius XII.

Crimthann's grandfather always burst into the same song at family weddings.

> No more he'll hear a seagull cry o'er the murmuring Shannon tide …
> A martyr for old Ireland, Seán South of Garryowen.

'Sit in the back and it will be a longer journey,' said a man in a flat cap on the bus going to Stranraer, 'Life is not easy. You make plans and there's a hitch. It never turns out the way you think it will.'

The bus broke down at Salford but there was a mechanic on board.

Later there was a pitched battle between some passengers at a transport café.

Crimthann crossed from Stranraer to Larne. There'd been some boys in the blue of Glasgow Rangers on the boat.

He'd always wanted to see Windsor Park, home of Linfield Football Club, who wore emerald green.

'Lillibulero' was sung by the Apprentice Boys after the Siege of Derry in 1689.

It was sung by the victors after the Battle of the Boyne in 1690.

In London, ladies had the tune printed on their fans.

It was still occasionally sung after soccer matches at Windsor Park, as it had been on the Cregagh estate, Belfast, where George Best, whose grandfather was a Protestant hurler in the Glens of Antrim, once kicked a plastic Frido ball, in a Davy Crockett cap.

'Lillibulero bullenala.'

Near Cregagh estate Crimthann purchased fish and chips wrapped in the *Shankill Mirror*, a wall painting to the side of the fish-and-chip shop with King Billy in a Quaker collar, on a Hanoverian cream horse.

Crimthann's father had been a George Best lookalike when young.

George Best, taken from his home at fifteen to join a team that originated in Newton Heath, an Irish Catholic area of Manchester.

First, Irish Catholic players had to change half a mile from the soccer pitch in the Three Crowns public house.

George Best used to score with his head.

Would meet his Irish Catholic colleagues, Nobby Stiles and

Paddy Crerand, outside a Roman Catholic church in Manchester on Sunday mornings.

Announced his retirement at twenty-six.

Sent off at Southampton a few years after his retirement for foul and abusive language.

Awarded a red card for obstreperousness.

Like Jack Doyle, he toured English provincial theatres, in his case telling soccer stories.

Crimthann's father had told Crimthann this soccer story: when Norman Whiteside, the Shankill Road skinhead, the youngest-ever player in the World Cup, kissed Kevin Moran, former Dublin Gaelic champion, after Manchester United's victory against Everton in the FA finals in 1985, his ikon was universally taken down on the Shankill Road.

Crimthann took a Goldliner bus to Dublin, a Lonsdale bag slung over his shoulder.

A poster of Coventry City's six-foot-one Gary Breen with Minnie Mouse side-hair was brought back from England.

Crimthann had seen a picture of Gary Breen in a McNicholls' hut in Thornton Heath, a postcard of Lifford, County Donegal, beside it, where Shay Given was from, who now played in Newcastle magpie.

Gary Breen's father was from County Kerry. Mother from south-west Clare where gannets make white flame against the sea.

Grandfather, Des, won an All-Ireland Gaelic football medal in 1913.

Himself a child of Kentish Town.

As a boy Gary Breen played centre forward for Westwood Boys in Camden Town.

Some boys from Camden Town used to make a pilgrimage to Walsingham at the beginning of June each year in soccer shorts and Puma football boots, passing through Horsham St Faith where St Robert Southwell was from and after the pilgrimage play soccer on the beach by Wells-next-the-Sea.

Generations of Irish immigrants had knelt in despair before the image of Our Lady of Walsingham in her pomegranate dress and three-pronged crown curled at the end like Arabian slippers.

Camden Town boys in their soccer shorts would present bunches of Spanish bluebells or red campion or shining cranesbill or marsh orchids, picked along the way, to her.

As a Westwood Boys centre forward Gary Breen got a tumour in his lower spine. It was cut away in hospital. He was unable to walk properly for a year and had difficulty sleeping. The doctors told his parents he'd never play football again but within a few years he'd signed on with Gillingham.

His grandmother in Clare lit candles from Lourdes and candles blessed on St Brigid's Day when he was playing.

A week before the Second World War broke out, when men emigrated from Ireland with their belongings wrapped in brown paper under their arms, an IRA bomb killed five people in Coventry.

In February 1940, James McCormick and Peter Barnes were hanged in Winson Green Prison, Birmingham, for a bombing it was subsequently proved they didn't do.

> Plow the land with the horn of a lamb
> Parsley, sage, rosemary, and thyme,
> Then sow some seeds from north of the dam
> And then he'll be a true love of mine.

Crimthann's twenty-first birthday was the following summer.

Earlier in the summer, on Lapp's Quay, he and his friends witnessed a pod of orca whales – the Demon Dolphin, Wolf of the Sea, black, grey saddle – bull, cow, female, which had come as far as City Hall, doing spy-hops and tail-slaps there.

There was a ricepaper photograph in the middle of Crimthann's cake of Crimthann in the signal-red jersey with butterfly-cream sleeves of Arsenal.

Flahri, Afro hair – Irish mother, cuckoo Libyan father, father who ran away – with a miniature ArmaLite rifle on a chain around his neck, which he says was a gift, sang Phil Colclough's 'Song for Ireland'.

Daire, one of Crimthann's friends, on holiday from Germany, in a tank top that showed his tattoo – a leprechaun in tank top with the words 'Irish Power' beneath him – told a soccer story.

A donkey who was mistreated ran away and met a dog, a cat and a cockerel on the road in a similar predicament and they went together to Bayern – home of Bayern Leverkusen.

'They talk about the Birmingham Six or the Guildford Four,' Crimthann says as a lighted tanker passes from the Shannon estuary to the Atlantic, 'but there are other Irish incarcerations in England that are not known or heard of, people who had to leave, who feel they had to leave, who couldn't face home, who ended up in their own prisons in England, unwanted, outcast, barely tolerated, neglectful of themselves, holding on only to a few items – pictures on the wall of Gary Breen or Princess Di.

'There are so many prisons in England and the prisons are Irish people who live in loneliness and isolation and abandonment and even self-torture – knowing they can never go back, that there's been some crime, some unforgivable sin ...'

Sweet Marjoram

Lowden, in black, pulled-down woollen cap and cream chinos, drives me to the ocean after class in his Malibu Chevrolet.

He is a Chinese boy, a karate champion, born in Toronto, his parents from Taiwan. They moved to the Bay Area when he was a child and later to southern California.

Lowden visited Taiwan recently when the pearl cherries were ripe, and despite the fact he speaks Chinese they asked who the American was.

He feels lost, lonely in the States, he says. And he adds:

'We live in an evil time.'

He's got to meet his American girlfriend who wears orange-brick lipstick and I say I'd like to stay on the beach and go for a swim.

He leaves and I swim.

A drunken man in an ox-blood lumber jacket, chaperoned by two young sons, one in bermudas with a pattern of golfing appendages, the other in bermudas with chickens on bicycles on them, looks on.

'You'll freeze your ass.'

'Dad, come on.' His children lead him away.

'Give peace in our time, O Lord,' goes a prayer in the Book of Common Prayer and, as a sandpiper flies against the biblical papaya of the sky, I think of Lady Tamar Strathnairn and how she tells of the time I live in.

I was sitting at a terrace table on Museum Street in the summer of 1977 when she approached me in a white shift dress and dark-cherry ballet slippers.

Her jaw-length hair was japanned-black and her skin ultra-white.

A Boadicea with a beehive was arranging vegetables at the British Museum side of the street as Lady Tamar spoke to me.

I'd just come back from southern Europe and I was wearing the knee-high boots I'd bought in an Ottoman alley in Hania.

In Marktplatz in Heidelberg on my way back I'd bumped into a friend from Cork who, in an Elizabethan Irishwoman's cloak, fastened with a fibula and falling in folds to the ground, was busking with her guitar, and I bottled for her in sea-cerulean dungarees.

The song she sang most frequently was 'Only Our Rivers Run Free'.

An American lady, with saffron-rinsed hair, in black trouser-suit and peep-toe cut-out sandals, wept.

My friend and I had an Italian meal beside Heidelberger Schloss with the proceeds.

'Let the dead bury the dead,' she whispered by candlelight so she looked like Correggio Zingarella's 'Gypsy Girl'.

I attended Lady Tamar's supper in a flat near the Russian embassy for which Lady Tamar wore a stretch-lamé tube dress with a caterpillar brooch on it, which had purple stone eyes.

Her other guest was a youth in an Orator Hunt red neckerchief and red Stuart tartan trousers.

He was an official in the Troops Out movement.

Her father was a high-ranking officer who moved between Ebrington Barracks, Derry; Gough Barracks, Armagh; Royal Inniskilling Fusiliers, Omagh.

Her mother worked for the administration of the Church of England.

Tamar had a job as a secretary in an art gallery in Mayfair.

On the wall was a reproduction of *Venus and Adonis* by Christian van Cowenbergh; Adonis with hippie-length hair, Venus with parure in her strawberry-blonde hair.

At the beginning of my travels in the summer I'd stopped at Plâs Newydd at Llangollen in Wales to visit the home of Lady Eleanor Butler, who'd run away with Sarah Ponsonby from the banks of the Nore in County Kilkenny in 1778, Eleanor aged thirty-nine, Sarah aged twenty-three; black-and-white marble-stoned floor, coloured oriel window, Gothic-crossed timber outside – where I met a boy in a multi-coloured woollen jersey.

'If you're a Taffy and wearing a pendant you're alright,' he said to me.

Lady Eleanor used wear the Bourbon Croix de Saint-Louis around her neck.

A fat girl, who frequently wore a lady's horned medieval hat, and a thin boy who said he was from West Mercia – western midlands – were having a bath together on the street of squats I lived in, lit by a scented candle, to John McLaughlin's 'Swan on Irish Waters', reading passages of George Borrow's *Lavengro* to one another, from a copy stolen from Wandsworth Library, when the ceiling fell down.

'There's a great sadness in you,' a fellow squatter, with a palmer's haircut, in Robin Hood hose stockings, said to me, by candlelight so he looked like Gerrit van Honthorst's *Christ Before the High Priest* I'd just seen at the National Gallery.

There were boys in the squat who played Little John and William Scathelock to this Robin Hood.

Some of them left the squat to go to a commune of screamers on an island off County Mayo – people who screamed for therapy.

Lady Tamar frequently visited me now that I was back in London, still in my knee-high boots from Crete.

I shared a room with a boy with a ruby-auburn cockscomb from County Kerry, whose father used to bathe him in the Smearla – blackberry – River, whose National School teacher used to give him the ass's bite – clench in the groin.

We slept on mattresses on the floor.

Late one night he told me about a friend.

A boy who was an electrician from Athlone, Correggio's shepherdboy, Ganymede, or Murillo's young St Thomas of Villanueva, who's distributing his clothes to poor boys, in hipster jeans and pip necklace.

On the way to Berlin from Ireland, he'd slept in a house of labourers in Dollis Hill. He had to share a bed with one of the labourers and he touched the labourer's penis. For him a sacrosanct gesture. But the labourer went around telling everyone:

'He touched my Seán Thomas.'

The basking shark and the porbeagle shark and the blue shark would draw in sight of my room-mate's part of Kerry in the autumn after shoals of herring.

'Can I sleep with you?' he asked one night, displaying his mouse's nest pubic area. He got into bed beside me.

In bed he told me this story:

Near his home in Kerry were sea caves.

During the Civil War a group of Irregulars hid in them. The Free Staters smoked them out by throwing down burning bales of hay. Subsequently they cut a rope and three of the Irregulars were drowned in the rising tide.

But a survivor turned out to be a young Englishman, a deserter from the British army.

Next morning Lady Tamar arrived in a black kaftan and top hat, with a pile of scarlet-rose blankets and Elizabeth Shaw Peppermint Creams.

When I was in Scotland in February, where I heard a cinnamon-haired boy in Barra sing 'The Gypsy Laddie', she came looking for me and slept with my friend.

They drove around London in her chocolate-and-cream Sun Singer convertible and went to a church hall near the squat to see a boy from Hayling Island do a thaumaturgic dance, with bare chest, in Turkish trousers, watched by white witches from Rochester, Sandgate, Havant, Herne Bay.

Shortly afterwards the boy from Kerry went to live in Milwaukee where some of his fellow county people still speak Irish.

> She gave them the good wheat bread,
> And they gave her the ginger,
> But she gave them a far better thing,
> The gold ring off her finger.

In May, when I lived in a room near St Paul's, Hammersmith, Lady Tamar sat with me through the night before I took a plane to New York.

She asked me why I never made love to her, was I gay?

Under a postcard of Goya's *The Forge*, full of biceps and male décolletage, I told her I'd been in love with a girl with narcissus-coloured hair, that a woman had attacked me at a party in Dublin and accused me of impotence.

Sexual harmony was ruptured; the hose of a Japanese ballet dancer in Madrid as it pressed on his genitals.

Against a postcard of Renoir's Alexander Thurneyssen as a young shepherd – rag hat, sheepskin, flute – Lady Tamar confided to me that a few years before she'd been in and out of mental hospitals.

She got these attacks sometimes.

Something hit her.

She took to walking the streets in a trance, in her mother's flat Second World War hat tilted to one side, studying shop signs or the numbers and manufacturers' names on pavement lids.

She was much better now.

A small group of young men with yeminis – painted handkerchiefs – around their necks playing Jewish violins in Central Park; then a Greyhound bus down Roman roads in Wyoming.

In the Patio Café on Castro Street, San Francisco, which was frequented by a red-breasted American house finch, my friend from Dublin told me she was getting married to a man who wore a blue ombré headband.

I went to Yosemite National Park after she told me, and half-way up Tuolumne Meadows, in a grove of blossoming bear garlic, I repeated to myself a bit of Native American history:

'Black Elk returned to Wounded Knee to mourn the butchered women and children.'

Autumn that year was a bunch of marigolds on a cabinet table under the glowing and sidelong face of Rembrandt's *Nicolaes Bruyning*, 1652.

Black Elk put on his ghost shirt before the Battle of Wounded Knee and in the next few years in London a ghost shirt was necessary.

Lady Tamar occasionally sent me At Home cards.

At these gatherings, which resembled John Tenniel's Mad Hatter's Tea Party, were guests from the art gallery and its world — young men in collarless suits, young lords named Meriwether or Redvers or Egerton who addressed you as Lord Emsworth might his pig, the Empress of Blandings.

One of these young lords said that Tamar looked like a London marchesa who used to make herself up to look like a corpse.

I taught in a comprehensive in South Kensington.

I brought them to Hampton Court, children from the stucco villas of Holland Park and the faubourgs of White City. Sad, adult-faced boys with pommelled hairstyles who cycled junior bicycles on the walkways of White City; blonde, troubador-haired boys with slightly stooped shoulders who smote your fists with their fingers.

A boy with kibbled hair called Elidore after a boy of Welsh legend told me how his mother, who was active in the Troops Out movement, living in a commune where she wore a floating evening gown patterned with double-humped camels, had disowned him, banging the door on him when he called to see her.

In early summer I brought them to Brighton beach and Tamar came too.

One of them — an Arab boy — wouldn't go into the water so I lifted him in his black silk shirt, napped black trousers, and dropped him into the sea, which that day was Medici blue.

She seemed to be forever going off on holidays to far-off places and she sent me postcards — flowering peach in Virginia; a bougainvillaea esplanade in Famagusta; a skiing slope in the Lebanon.

She even went to visit her father in Northern Ireland and sent me a postcard of William Conor's wax-crayon Belfast jaunting car; bowler-hatted jarvey, woman with deep-terracotta scarf holding a child wrapped in cinnabar red; little boy with girl-length hair, in army-green jersey, at the back, naked legs dangling.

Towns with no evangel but the Union Jack; a soldier who jogged every day by Lough Neagh with a backpack of bricks; Sunday service at Campbell College where William Conor, walking entirely in black through Belfast, was recalled; a young soldier doing a sailor's hornpipe in green hunting tartan; a swan on Irish waters.

Then she threw up her job in the art gallery and went to Cambridge as a late pupil for four years.

I visited her on a day trip.

As a student she had strangely become more conservative in her dress. She wore two-tone shoes, blue and cream, a deep-flared peplum jacket, divided skirt. There was a vintage rose in her cheeks.

In her flat in an isolated ivy-overgrown house by the River Cam she sat under a reproduction of Lucas Cranach's *The Virgin and Child Under an Apple Tree.*

Outside Cambridge station a man in Morris costume, bucket in hand, had been busking for the striking miners.

O eat your cherries, Mary,
O eat your cherries now,
O eat your cherries, Mary,
That grow upon the bough.

We had tea and almond-and-amaretto Madeira cake in a café near a cinema painted Reckitt's blue with posters for fifties British films in the foyer — *The Belles of St Trinian's, Carry on Sergeant, Dracula* — served by a waitress with pillar-box-red lipstick and afterwards in a church we listened to an Anglican canticle: 'There is no Health in Me'. In March 1985 the miner's strike ended.

After Cambridge she went to teach in a girls' public school near her family home in East Sussex, for which she donned half-moon rimless spectacles, and I was invited to her house for a weekend.

The baronial house with Tudor gables, dormer windows, had a lake beside it, a herringbone path leading there.

Dog wagons had once drawn wood from the nearby forest to this house and Gypsy children, with hair the colour of sunlit chestnuts, had come looking for partridge eggs in the hedgerows bordering the forest — olive and ochre, occasionally blueish-white, blotched with red ochre.

The white blossom of the wild service tree, the barren strawberry in spring; the blue pimpernel; the true fox sedge in summer; red berries of the butcher's broom in the forest in autumn — the Flora Annie Steel *Fairy Tales* of my childhood could have happened here.

I met Lady Tamar's mother.

Hair dressed away from her face, in vicuña slacks, mules.

With Bobbly, her cat, on her lap, seated on a scroll-ended sofa, Lady Tamar's mother, who was a winter swimmer — on winter weekdays she swam in the carpet of gold leaves in the Ladies' pond in Highgate with Jewish women who were survivors of Auschwitz, or in Leg of Mutton Pond in Hampstead — named feast days in her conversation to mark the year as a Russian might — St Lucy's Day, Ember Day, the Nativity of Saint John the Baptist, Midsummer's Day, when garlands of St John's wort are put on the door in East Sussex and you draw a circle around yourself with a rowan stick and poles of herbs are hoisted.

In the morning in the garden she showed me, beside the yellow calceolarias, a bed of sweet marjoram, and told me the story of Amaracus, a Greek youth at the court of the kings of Cyprus who, with a chaplet of vine leaves in his hair and in *all'antica* sandals, accidentally dropped a vessel containing perfume.

His terror on realizing the magnitude of his crime caused him to faint.

The gods, sparing him dire punishment, transformed him into a sweet-smelling plant named after him.

She plucked a bunch of burnt-orange chrysanthemums and gave them to me.

Shortly afterwards I was invited to the southern States.

In the southern States I lived in a carpenter's Gothic house, a weeping-fig tree outside it.

My first memory is of crossing water on a train. Yachts on the water. Was it somewhere near Bray, County Wicklow? Had it been a dream?

The only similar experience in my life, apart from the lagoon train to Venice, was the train that crosses the bridge over Lake Pontchartrain.

Strange the feeling of returning over that bridge in winter from New Orleans where troupes of boys in rubber shorts with the backs cut out did the cancan, where the Ursuline Sisters who delivered New Orleans by prayers to Our Lady of Prompt Succour during the Battle of New Orleans in 1815 still had the reward of free passage on the public transport system, to the winter Bible country – Covenanters' bungalows with dogtrots.

An Amaracus of a boy, with a Titus crop, in linted jeans, briefly told me his story.

He'd belonged to the wrong family. He'd travelled in a Ford Ranger with the American flag in front on dirt roads, on fire roads, from California.

Now he was with the right family.

On my return, London no longer seemed home.

I spent a few years going back and forth between London and Berlin, from which I sent Lady Tamar Martin Schongauer's *Nativity* – Rhinemaiden Madonna, cow with elk-like antlers – and she and I didn't meet and when those transits ceased and we did meet she had a pug-royal look.

There was grey in front of her hair the way Lady Eleanor Butler had put powder in front of her hair, her lipstick rose of Lancaster red.

She was living in London again, teaching there.

She was getting bad attacks again, wandering the streets in a scarlet coat dress and unstructured hat with wide turned-back brim, studying the pagodas in a travel poster or standing on benches in churches to examine the plaques.

Aristocratic ancestors, she told me, by way of explanation, had the task of carrying news of their coming executions to fellow aristocrats.

Screech owls, bloodhounds ...

In Berlin, just before I left, I saw a production of Schiller's *Mary Stuart*, in which Maria Stuart mounted the scaffold at the end:

'Constancy becomes all folks well, and none better than princes ...'

A stone came through my French windows in south-east London, where I'd lived for twelve years, shattering the glass over a mosaic of postcards from The Hermitage in St Petersburg – Luca Giordano's beefcake *Forge of Vulcan*; Veronese's *Pietà* with a red-headed man taking Christ's hand; Correggio's *Portrait of a Lady* – black dress, jewel in her hair, brown scapular of a Franciscan tertiary on her bosom ...

Portrait of a Lady ...

Lady Tamar often visited me in my last six months in London, in a room overlooking a noisy throughfare in Hampstead, and, just as when I first arrived, she brought cheese from Paxton and Whitfield's and Elizabeth Shaw Peppermint Creams.

Sometimes we went to swim in Highgate ponds. She'd go to the Ladies' pond and I'd go to the Men's.

On Saturdays and Sundays there were three boy late swimmers – Dominic, Ben and Stephen – who liked to stand around naked after their swim.

'Safe Des.'

'When parents break up who gets the custody of the hamster? The mother gets hold of it on weekdays. And the father at weekends.'

Afterwards, Lady Tamar and I would sit on a bench just above the Men's pond, dedicated to the memory of a young man, she in a thistle-printed crêpe-de-Chine blouse or a knitted jersey with appliqué kingfishers.

Anglican bells for the dead occasionally rang from St Anne's Church whose grounds abounded in ladybird-infested pyracantha.

When Keats, whose house was nearby, had been at school, the teacher, Rev. Clarke, would bring his pupils into the courtyard to see the departure of the swallows.

> Be careful ere ye enter in, to fill your baskets high
> With fennel green ...
> Cool parsley, basil sweet, and sunny thyme.

Lady Eleanor Butler – of one of the steadfast Catholic families of Ireland, whose cousin's house, Cill Chais in County Tipperary, was the subject of a poem learnt at National School, a lament for the great Catholic house by a young priest – had been devoted to a herb garden near the river Dee in Wales, which reminded her of the Nore in County Kilkenny, its wild privet banks, its yellow water-lily-covered water, its poppy-bordered river paths.

The tragic measure; Shakespeare was performed in the Kilkenny of Lady Eleanor Butler's girlhood.

My arm would go around Lady Tamar's shoulder for the affair we never had.

As autumn became late autumn an Amaracus in old-fashioned black bib swimming togs would walk out on the pier in the Men's pond to swim – just as boys do late in the year at the weir in Bishop's Meadows in Kilkenny with their distant view of St Canice's Cathedral – often against a late-afternoon sun that was as red-orange as Californian poppy.

The Hare's Purse

The old alchemists considered mercury the spirit, sulphur the soul, salt the body.

Sulphur united with mercury and salt for Seán South on the evening of January 1st 1957 – when County Monaghan country people say there's a cock step more light – with the burst of a Bren gun.

Fergal O'Hanlon – Fergal Máire (Mary) Ó hAnnluain – aged twenty, from Park Street, Monaghan town; Seán South – Seán Sabhat – aged twenty-nine, from Henry Street, Limerick: killed in a raid on Brookeborough police station, County Fermanagh, five miles over the Northern Ireland border, with twelve other men, four of them injured, one critically.

A Christian Brother with embonpoint, who taught at the Abbey CBS in Tipperary town, had once told Seán South, in the Royal Hotel by the willowherb-choked Ara River, Tipperary town, the story written in Greek by Lucian of Samosata about a group of adventurers who, as they sail through the Strait of Gibraltar, are lifted by a giant waterspout and deposited on the moon.

There they witness the war between the king of the moon and the king of the sun over the colonization rights of Jupiter, involving armies of stalk-and-mushroom men, acorn-dogs, cloud-centaurs, with the moon men, hit in combat, dissolving into smoke.

The Slieve Beagh mountain march by the twelve survivors through the hilly, boggy countryside between Brookeborough and the border took five hours.

Lights and flares of search parties lit up the countryside.

The County Donegal golden eagle was an occasional visitor to this mountain.

Doing a roller-coaster on sighting a hare, soaring upward to a point, then tucking its wings to descend at a speed of up to two hundred miles per hour.

Golden to blonde feathers at the neck; thus the name.

Chrysos being the Greek word for golden, the Tipperary-town Christian Brother once having informed Seán South.

Atropos being the Greek goddess who determined life or death, he added the same evening.

Atropos had determined death for Seán South and Fergal O'Hanlon that night.

But for the survivors, with the lights and flares it was like the battle on the moon frequently related in Irish by Seán South.

The Cortolvin Bridge over the old Ulster Canal was lined with people in Monaghan town awaiting Fergal O'Hanlon's hearse.

Woodland blue, bluebell – *cloigín gorm* – eyes, cheeks red as the little cup of the yew tree, lips like Joe Louis, teeth that lost a gold crown, chased tweed jackets with shamrock, primrose or *fáinne* – ring-shaped badge of the Irish Language Association – in lapel.

A draughtsman in Monaghan courthouse.

Played for Senior Monaghan Harps in their white and blue. In the shower had a body like a bunch of the garden plant, lamb's ears.

Coached Minor Monaghan Harps.

Remembered sitting on the edge of Gavan Duffy Park, instructing young players.

Gavan Duffy, from Dublin Street, Monaghan town, the only Irish rebel knighted by Queen Victoria.

Chiefly remembered in Monaghan town for having had four children in his seventies.

Hearse passed Magnet Cinema on Glaslough Street – four-penny, eight-penny, shilling seats – where *Rebel Without a Cause* had very recently been shown.

James Dean in wine-coloured zip-up jacket and azure skinny jeans.

A blue-and-white long-distance coach having taken Dean from Chicago Greyhound Bus Station to southern California where he gained the confidence to shed his gawky Hoosier Indiana adolescence and emerge like this.

Fergal's coffin was taken off the hearse outside St Louis Convent, where exchanging manicure sets was then in vogue, and borne through Monaghan town by youths with shellacked cockscombs, farmhands' cockscombs, slicked-back hair like James Dean, or the Levee (the Panama) – back-sweep and crest, greased side-boards.

They'd all seen the colour-drenched chickie run in *Rebel Without a Cause* – car race towards cliff edge, jumping out at the last moment.

Bearers of the coffin halted in front of the O'Hanlon home in Park Street – his mother's name, Darby, linked her by a marriage to Tommy Donnelly, commandant of Fifth Northern Division, Old IRA – while a tricolour flew from a window.

Seán South, a clerk at MacMahon's timber firm in Limerick city – hair the ginger of the ginger daub at the top of a mushroom, with side-combed crest and back-swept sides, eyes low-tide blue, earnest glasses.

He'd been compared for his very serious expression to Stewart Granger in *King Solomon's Mines*, based on Henry Rider Haggard's novel.

The hearse followed on O'Connell Street, Dublin, under Player's Please and Jacob's Chocolates advertisements, by Fianna Éireann – olive-green uniforms and cocked hats like the Ancient Order of Foresters who used to sing patriotic songs in nineteenth-century Dublin music halls.

It was raining heavily as the hearse arrived at the Old County Hospital, Dublin Road, Portlaoise, as part of its nine-and-a-half-hour journey from Dublin to Limerick city.

His widowed mother met the hearse in Roscrea.

Eleven thousand marched and eleven thousand lined the streets in Limerick city.

Twenty prominent religious leaders, city and county councillors, senators, a member of parliament, the Forty-Ninth Battalion of
the FCA — Local Defence Force — bus- and garage-men, Gaelic football and hurling teams, Gaelic League, Old Irish Volunteers, Nationalist Women's Society, followed the hearse past Spillane's who made
Garryowen Plug tobacco.

Curragower Falls on Shannon in torrent.

A busker heard to play 'Father Murphy of Old Kilcormac' and
'Don't Forget Your Dear Old Mother' on mouth organ.

Never known to sing or play a violin in Limerick city, Seán
South had played a violin as a lady played on piano, and afterwards
sang 'Eibhlín A Rún' — Eileen So Coy — in Monaghan town a few
days prior to the attack on Brookeborough police station.

The IRA of the 1950s consisted of mavericks — carpenters or
plumbers with artistic inclinations who'd launch into a ballad in the
box snug of a pub with cartoons outside of an ostrich snatching a
glass of Guinness from a Royal Irish Constabulary man in his rifle
green, or Royal Irish Constabulary men in the same rifle green with
their caps popping in the air as a pelican makes off with their Guinness bottles in his beak, or a tortoise transporting a pint of Guinness.

Dearg-ghráin — intense hatred — was the attitude to England.

Because of this *dearg-ghráin*, the brother of novelist Edith
Somerville — white lisle dresses, bow ties, who'd seen the *Titanic* pass
west Cork and the corpses washed in from the *Lusitania* as her gingham
umbrella was raised — was murdered when he answered the door at
The Point, Castletownsend, west Cork, on the evening of 24 March
1936, for writing references for farmers' sons with marigold and buttercup hair who wished to join the Royal Navy.

These IRA men — some of whom were known to dress in
apricot jackets with triple wooden buttons at cuffs, ultramarine
shirts, lizard-skin pumps — could recite the poem by north Leinster
Séamus Dall Mac Cuarta about the King-Badger who loved not
pleasure, or the poem by County Fermanagh Cathal Buí Mac Giolla
Ghunna about the yellow bittern who, for all the vanity of its
powder-down feather, died of thirst, laid out like the ruin of Troy,

water voles at its wake, clearly showing the importance of being frequently drunk because there wouldn't be drink when you're dead!

The Irish language is an encyclopaedia of oppression.

Seán South, who grew a beard in his last month and swore he wouldn't shave it until the Six Counties were free, was forever quoting a line by Angus Mac Daighre Ó Dálaigh:

> Ag seilg troda ar fhéinn eachtrann
> Gá bhuil fearrann bhur sinnsear.
> (Urging fight against the foreign soldiery that
> holds your fatherland.)

Eachtrann being foreign.
Eachtraí being —
Storyteller. Traveller. Exile.

Storyteller. Traveller. Exile.

One song is built on the ruin of another the way the swallow builds its mud saucer on a spotted flycatcher's domed house.

A song was quickly written about puppy-faced Fergal to the air of 'The Merry Month of May':

> Was in the merry month of May
> When flowers were a bloomin'.

In another version of Barbara Allan:

> Since my love died for me today,
> I'll die for him tomorrow.

Fergal's song was made internationally famous by an American lady singer who wore headbands with patterns of snowshoe hares or lobster moths and by a scrannel-voiced American male singer with a gun-shot expression.

The songwriter was best man at the Brookeborough column commander's — Pearse column after the 1916 revolutionary — wedding and the song accompanied the songwriter to the grave because that Pearse column commander gave the oration at his graveside.

A song was also quickly written about Séan South to the air of 'Roddy McCorley':

> Young Roddy McCorley goes to die
> On the bridge at Toome today.

But that song, which was very often sung with 'The Boys of Bluehill', only had an Irish audience.

> We are the boys who take delight
> In smashing Limerick lamps at night.

It was a Limerick song – 'The Boys of Garryowen' – that General Custer's Seventh Cavalry Regiment sang as they left General Terry's column at Powder River.

Garryowen a district in Limerick city around St John's Cathedral and an affectionate name for Limerick city.

'The Boys of Garryowen' a Royal Irish Regiment marching song.

The Royal Irish Regiment celebrated for valour at the Battle of Namur in 1695 where one of William of Orange's lieutenants used Capuchin friars as spies.

Met, on the opposite side, some of their former comrades who'd opted to go with the Wild Geese – Irish soldiers who exiled themselves in Europe after the Treaty of Limerick, 1691 – at the Battle of Malplaquet, 1709, during the War of Spanish Succession.

Custer heard a Royal Irish Regiment emigrant sing the song while drunk at Fort Riley, Kansas.

The United States had previously known the Royal Irish Regiment when they'd been garrisoned at the Illinois Country until they fought at Lexington, Concord and Bunker Hill during the American War of Independence.

The Royal Irish Regiment was present at Yorktown, Virginia, 1781, when the triumphant Americans played 'Yankee Doodle', 'Redcoats' and 'The World Turned Upside Down', a children's rhyme from the English Civil War:

> Derry down, down, hey derry down,
> I am come to make peace in this desperate fray.

Fergal O'Hanlon, born Candlemas Day – Candelmaesse – 1936.

Candlelight processions to the altar to commemorate the purification of Mary and presentation of Christ at the Temple began 381–4 AD.

The following month German troops reoccupied the demilitarized Rhineland in violation of the Treaty of Versailles.

At the Christian Brothers' School, Monaghan town, he learnt that a Monaghan-town man, General Don Juan McKenna, was one of the founders of Chile.

A De La Salle brother from Limerick came and tried to take him to the De La Salle Brothers in Limerick when he was fourteen.

But his destiny was to excel at Latin at St Macartan's College.

Caesar Augustus forbade boys to run during the Lupercalia festival, who hadn't shaved off their first beards.

Boys without their first beards played football in the black-and-amber jerseys of St Macartan's College and in tube football togs – togs down to their knees met by black-and-amber calf socks.

By the Blackwater the lesser celandine – *grán arcáin* (piglet's grain) – grew.

In the summer the foxglove in profusion.

> Méirín puca.
> Méirín sí.
> Méirín dearg.
> (Hobgoblin finger.
> Fairy finger.
> Red finger.)

Boys whose first pubic hair was like the buff dust on the dark-brown wood argus butterfly's wing swam in the Blackwater at Patton's Mill.

There was a school day trip to see the tympanum of Portland stone in the Cathedral of Christ the King in Mullingar, where the canal ended; of Pope Pius XI; the Most Reverend Thomas Mulvany, Bishop of Meath; Cardinal MacRory, Primate of All Ireland.

Working for Monaghan County Council, Fergal would tie children's shoelaces on the street, lift children on his broad shoulder.

He trained with the FCA rifle practice.

Remembering nineteen-year-old IRA volunteer Thomas Williams

hanged by the Northern Ireland government during the Second World War, despite the pleas of the lord mayor of Dublin, the Dublin Fire Brigade and the people of Achill Island, County Mayo.

Christmas 1955, Fergal inscribed in an autograph book a Horace epigram massively popular with the British Empire during the Boer War:

'Sweet and appropriate thing to die for one's country.'

Christmas 1956, wrote in his diary:

'Keep cool and pray. A good conscience is a continual Christmas.'

The song about him is about an IRA *Bildungsroman* — a young person's education.

He'd been a member of the IRA for two years before volunteering for column work. It was a secret in Monaghan town that he was in the IRA.

At parochial-hall dances he led girls to Teresa Brayton's 'The Old Bog Road'.

On his death a number of Monaghan-town girls left to be nuns in the Dominican Convent, Portstewart, County Derry, and with the Sisters of St Francis Xavier in Omagh, County Tyrone.

Seán South's home, 47 Henry Street, had been a synagogue when it was the home of a draper, Louis Goldberg, a blonde Lithuanian who escaped conscription into the Russian army by taking a timber ship to Ireland where, after obtaining a pedlar's licence for ten shillings, he began by selling pictures of saints and popes.

Limerick Jews, mainly from the village of Akmijan, province of Kovna Gubernia, Lithuania, were a familiar sight, eating ginger butter cakes, poppyseed butter cakes, sugar pretzels under the walnut blossom, the kanzan cherry blossom, the ornamental red hawthorn, the sweet chestnut trees in Pery Square park.

Shortly after Chanukkah, feast of lights, early 1904, year of the canonization of Gerard Majella, a Jewish wedding for which the bride had a bouquet of white carnations and maidenhair fern, the bridesmaids' satin capes trimmed with swan's down, green marzipan and candied orange slices served at the feast, inspired the wrath of Father John Creagh, in a city where the lice of the poor were so large they caused Father Creagh's Redemptorists to vomit.

Father John Creagh – biretta, incised Limerick mouth, arched brows, melancholy dreaming eyes.

As director of the Archconfraternity of the Holy Family, from the pulpit Father Creagh accused the Jews of deicide.

April of the subsequent boycott, Jewish businesses were collapsing. Sophia Weinronk, out to get food, was attacked on Bowman Street, off Colooney Street – Jewish street of transoms and railings – her head beaten against the wall.

A poor herdsman's daughter in the hills of Shanagolden declared that only for Jews she would have no clothes or covering.

The parish priest of Kilcolman and Coolcappa made her return two blankets she'd just bought from a travelling Jewish draper, also from Henry Street.

Back in Limerick, Father Creagh claimed a Jew had tried to sell him a music-hall broadsheet with 'Squeeze Her Gently' on it.

Boherbuoy Brass and Reed Band led the superior general of Redemptorists from the station in July.

Confraternity salute was raised, right hand.

Papal blessing was given in three instalments – Monday, Tuesday to men, Wednesday to boys.

The pleas of Rabbi Elias Bere Levin from Tels, Lithuania, reached deaf ears.

Eighty Jews were driven from Limerick. Forty left.

Ginsbergs left. Jaffes left. Weinronks followed Greenfields to South Africa.

The Hebrew headstones survived in Kilmurry Cemetery, near Castleconnell.

'Why shouldst thou be as a stranger in the land and as a wayfaring man that turneth aside to tarry for a night?'

In Seán South's room in 47 Henry Street were bottles of Indian ink, paintbrushes, pens.

In the bookcase works by Charles Kickham, Canon Sheehan, Henry Rider Haggard, *Biggles* books, *The Little Prince* by the French aviator Antoine de Saint-Exupéry, with Sainte-Exupéry's drawing of the little prince in a jumpsuit with flared trousers and bow tie on the jacket.

A statue of the Sacred Heart wrapped in cellophane on top of it.

The Messenger of the Sacred Heart, Irish School Weekly.

A postcard of *The Race of the Gael* by Seán Keating – who'd painted a portrait of Bishop Edward Thomas O'Dwyer who settled a pork butcher's strike, a Mass said for him each year attended by pork butchers – two men staring with determination over a stone wall.

Gramophone records, Pat Roche's Harp and Shamrock Orchestra, The Pride of Erin Orchestra, 'O Sole Mio' by Enrico Caruso.

Seán South was a member of numerous organizations.

He founded a Limerick branch of Maria Duce in 1949, an organization with an anti-Semitic past – originated in the 1940s by the Very Reverend Dr Denis Fahey of the Holy Ghost Fathers, now targeting Hollywood actors inclined towards communism.

Member of the Gaelic League – Friends of the Irish Language – campaigned to have Irish spoken again on the streets of Limerick.

Member of Pacemakers of Freedom – a nationalist organization.

Of An Réalt – the star – an organization dedicated to the Virgin Mary.

One of his drawings is of Mary of Perpetual Help. In the words of St Ambrose, Mary, the Temple of God.

Pope Pius IX had sent an ikon of Our Lady of Perpetual Help to the Limerick Redemptorists in 1866, when the first Redemptorists in Ireland were being brought to court for burning Protestant Bibles.

Seán South vehemently campaigned against the Jehovah's Witnesses, one out of four having lost their lives in the Germany of the Third Reich; through constant litigation in the USA causing the Fourth Amendment to be more clearly defined, thus safeguarding the rights of all.

He studied drawing by doing an English art-school postal course – 'Which is the best way of demolishing a bridge?' – his last cartoon shows a beefcake IRA man guarding a classroom, an RUC man batoning the B-Special pupil beside him, another pupil in scanty mid-thigh shorts.

The drawings Antoine de Saint-Exupéry did to accompany *The*

Little Prince, written in a rented house in New York in 1943, helped Seán South to develop his drawing style, such as Saint-Exupéry's one of the conceited man with auguste's nose.

At fifteen, in the year *The Little Prince* was written, Seán South enlisted in the Auxiliary Army Force, which supplemented the Irish army during the Second World War, having darker-than-ordinary uniforms.

Two-hour FCA session per week.

Became a sergeant in the FCA proper April 1946 and became skilful in archery.

Out of the FCA, IRA full-time in April 1955 just after the premiere of *East of Eden* in which, against Californian clapboard, James Dean wears a sleeveless jersey with collegiate diamond pattern, his hair brushed up, the still of which quickly reached Limerick.

But Seán South's favourite organization was Servants of Freedom — boys with their first patina of body hair, between ten and fourteen.

The boys would have iced buns with hundreds and thousands — sugar strands — on them, kitsch queen cakes with thick pink icing, viridian jellies buried in the icing or tiny stars on it or, at Christmas, glittering studs, and tea from rose-patterned cups in a room with chocolate-indulgence-patterned wallpaper and a picture of Romulus and Remus, two putti who founded Rome, being borne on a wolf's back, in gilt frame with beaded edge.

Football, hurling, handball.

Recitations such as Sigerson Clifford's 'The Ballad of the Tinker's Daughter'.

Cartoon strips by Seán South for them in their magazine — *The Servant* — featuring Conor Mac Neasa and Cúchullain with cross-gartered legs.

Cromwell's second-in-command, Ireton, came to Limerick in 1651.

A children's rhyme from the English Civil War:

> If ponies rode men and if grass ate the cows ...
> If the mamas sold their babies
> To the Gypsies for half a crown ...
> Derry down, down, hey derry down.

Seán South brought his boys on an outing to identify estuarine reeds near the castle of Gerald, Earl of Desmond, who survived on horseflesh with sixty gallowglasses (Scottish mercenaries) during the Munster Rebellion in Elizabethan days until they tracked him down and beheaded him in a Kerry wood – the yellow bittern (*an bonnán buí*) of Cathal Buí Mac Giolla Ghunna's poem.

Ordinarily like a hen but it can make itself reed-like, by pointing its bill and body upward, as camouflage.

Voice of a cow who has lost her calf.

Dearg-ghráin.

Seán South told his boys that the favourite meal of Henry VIII of England was the innocent yellow bittern.

Seán South was renowned in Limerick for driving snogging couples from cinemas.

When *One Million BC* with a fur-clad Victor Mature was showing at Grand Central.

Cecil B. DeMille's *Samson and Delilah* at the Lyric with Hedy Lamarr's bellybutton inspiring epidemic snogging.

Demetrius and the Gladiators at the Savoy with Susan Hayward in peplum.

Athena with Dick DuBois in pristine white swimming trunks on the deck of a ship at the Thomond near Donkey Ford's Chipper. 'You'll end up in a Magdalene Laundry,' he was heard to say on that occasion to the girl in question, Magdalene Laundries being where unmarried pregnant girls were sent to labour.

But he brought his Servants of Freedom to *Lady and the Tramp* at the City Theatre.

Vegetables were scarce during the war, butter ration reduced, bacon limited.

The tasks of the volunteer soldiers in their forage caps and uniforms with chromium buttons were cattle-burying, turf-cutting.

Cut the turf in May with a slean – turf-spade – branch it, spread it.

In June the first footing. In July the second footing.

Then to Finner Camp in Donegal.

Michelangelos of young soldiers in the Atlantic; reddish-brown pubic hair in the showers, like the hare's coat; ice cream, swimming rings, toffee stands on Bundoran beach; Painted Lady butterflies with white marks on the black tips of the forewings on soldiers' black boots; tufted sedge, flat sedge, meadow foxtails, fuchsia reflected in young soldiers' torso tans, face freckles; ladybirds — scarabaeids — on young soldiers' forearms, in bronze hair.

Ladybird.

(*Bóin samhraidh*.

Cow of summer.)

French children tell the ladybird the Turks are coming to kill their children.

The Turks were coming then.

A man broadcast from Germany in Irish, continually reminding the Irish people that Germany had cooperated with the Shannon hydroelectric scheme near Limerick city in the late 1920s, the progress of which was painted by Seán Keating.

Before the war Glasgow prostitutes used to come to the environs of Finner Camp — thus it was known as the Scotch Fair.

But without the Glasgow prostitutes there was another kind of longing, like the hare's cry in the night.

Early August the volunteer soldiers would bring turf to towns and villages in County Limerick.

The Donie Collins Band toured County Limerick at harvest time during the war years, playing in dancehalls owned by farmers.

Packets of tea and cups were brought to them during an interval, in Jacob's biscuit tins.

The touring cinemas came then also — marquees in which films were shown — and stayed for a week.

Three Stooges films were particularly popular.

Canachán — hare's purse.

Working on the turf the volunteer soldiers slept under canvas.

Where hares grazed, checking the growth of grass, the large blue butterfly thrived — black spots on upper side of forewing — laying its eggs on wild thyme.

It had other secret, iridescent colours as its wings absorbed all the colours of the spectrum except blue.

The race of the Gael.

There were young soldiers' eyes like that.

The Arctic hare and the mountain hare of Europe turned white in winter.

But a young soldier, with bounty of chestnut hair and a metropolis of freckles on his face, from Lough Mask, County Mayo, where Lord Haw Haw, to whom Hitler awarded the War Merit Cross First Class, was from, told Seán South that in Mayo there were albino hares – white year-round.

The colonization rights of Jupiter …

The IRA campaign of 1956 began in December with a failed attempt to blow up the statue of General Gough on his horse in the Phoenix Park, Dublin.

Newspapers announced that some IRA men had been arrested at the border and were being detained by gardaí.

Headquarters was phoned.

The garda in charge warranted no ammunition had been found on them.

Whereupon instructions were that the IRA men be released.

The IRA men refused to be released because they'd abandoned their vehicle.

The garda in charge immediately ordered taxis and they were brought to Dublin for Christmas.

A garda in Limerick found a dock labourer from St Ita's Street in a car on Christmas Eve clasping a stolen plum pudding, value five shillings, and a stolen shoe, value fifteen shillings.

'Pray for me,' were Seán South's last words before leaving Limerick, with a bottle of Lourdes water.

Storyteller. Traveller. Exile.

In Dublin he attended a pantomime – *geamaire* – in which Jimmy O'Dea and Harry O'Donovan played the dames.

In the Monte Carlo Chipper in Monaghan town was a photograph of Gene Vincent and his Blue Caps – after President Eisenhower's baby-blue golf cap.

Four Blue Caps, who included Jumpin' Jack Neal and Wee Willie Williams, in black shirts and white ties; Gene Vincent, who shot swans as a boy in the swamps of Virginia for food, in a letterman jacket.

Gene Vincent had been fined ten thousand dollars the previous May by Virginia State Court because of a phoenetic error.

'Hugging on his Woman Love', because of all the moaning and panting, was mistaken for another word.

In keeping with the name of the chipper, Edith Piaf was playing on the jukebox – 'Les Trois Cloches' (Three Bells. Little Jimmy Brown. In the valley the bells are ringing).

Outside the Magnet Cinema a Teddy boy with floral-design cuffs was combing his hair with a metal comb.

A Marlborough Street magistrate, sentencing three Teddy boys for assault, had recently declared that their drainpipe trousers were a pity, because it made them difficult to pull down and give the boys a hiding.

In Dublin Street, Monaghan town, Gavan Duffy had been inspired by James Clarence Mangan's translations from medieval Irish.

In famine-striken Ireland state prisoners of Kilmainham Gaol subscribed three shillings and ten pence to Mangan when he descended into destitution.

Swans in the swamps of Virginia.

There were many swans in Monaghan because of all the lakes. Each lake with a narrative. Even the Convent Lake in Monaghan town had a narrative because there was a crannóg in it – a man-made island, a lake dwelling.

In the Pearse column, in squaddie's denims, with blackened face, Seán South's every order was given in Irish, then translated by him on the way to Brookeborough in a stolen council truck with tipper, which Sten guns would not penetrate, through lake countryside, through Scots pine – *giúis Albanach* – countryside.

He'd visited Patrick Pearse's cottage in Connemara, August 1954, and in his last hours he proclaimed about establishing Northern Ireland – where people watched *Dixon of Dock Green* on television, X-certificate films in the cinema, and listened to *Mrs Dale's Diary* and *The Archers* on radio – as a gaeltacht (Irish-speaking region).

At Brookeborough police station out rushed the assailants with a mine. Juice turned on.

Nothing happened.

A second installed. Failed.

Attempt to lob hand grenades through the barracks windows.

The previous year Seán South had visited many RUC barracks along the border to assess armaments. In Brookeborough he'd seen only pistols and Sten guns in the RUC arsenal, which was on open display.

A Bren gun was kept in married quarters upstairs.

An RUC sergeant opened fire with this Bren.

Seán South stayed by the Pearse column Bren until they riddled him.

He'd emptied three magazines into the barracks.

Small Fergal, as the Pearse column called him – he was five-foot, six-inches – was shot in the back and thighs.

The RUC Bren burst through the right door, roof, floor of stolen council truck. Tipper kept rising.

Bullet caught driver's foot.

Lights of a police patrol car down the road on their left as they made a getaway.

When the police patrol car was one hundred yards from them it opened fire.

At Altwark Cross, between Brookeborough and Rosslea, they stopped at a farmhouse.

Two Pearse column men went to the door. Knocked.

No reply.

One got in through the back. In the kitchen was a picture of the Sacred Heart.

They brought Seán and Fergal to an outhouse where a light was on. Under the light an act of contrition was whispered in Seán's ear.

Wounded column commander volunteered to stay.

Second-in-command ordered him away.

Fergal, Seán, truck abandoned.

But people in a nearby farmhouse, where there were Stygian greyhounds, asked to get a priest and doctor.

Police and B-Specials shot up farmhouse and outhouse.

Fergal died in a last burst of fire. Bled to death from a wounded thigh.

Since my love died for me today,
I'll die for him tomorrow.

Bren guns were mounted on the wall of Fermanagh County Hospital, Enniskillen, where the inquest was told that Seán South's head was bruised and discoloured.

Six survivors carried four wounded across Slieve Beagh.

Frequently they were forced to lie down because of the lights and flares. A compass guided them.

The bittern laid out like the ruin of Troy; hair turned white that night like the Arctic hare or the mountain hare of Europe in winter.

CinemaScope – letterbox screen – launched with *The Robe* starring Victor Mature and Jean Simmons, distorted faces, squeezed them.

Panavision improved this.

That night was in Panavision.

The House of Mourning

A stored digital photograph on a mobile phone; boy, tall, in off-white tank top, hair newly dyed, olive-gold, against the Shannon estuary in north Kerry, sea rocks shaped like manatees on which occasional blue fulmars spray a foul and oily substance.

He stands like a young guillemot about to parachute from a cliff nest to the sea.

In the theatre of another mobile phone the same boy in pale-blue Samsung-mobile-phone Chelsea T-shirt, a silver pendant around his neck, which is a replica of a silver pendant found near the second-century Hadrian's Wall in the north of England.

Rihanna's — Barbados girl of Irish descent — 'Unfaithful' plays for a few seconds on the same mobile phone.

'There was a mink on the Nun's Strand! I swear on my mother's life.'

Was the mink he saw Canadian or European? European minks had a white mark above the mouth. Both Canadian and European had a white mark below the mouth. Hard to see.

The mink would wait by the montbretia rushes for prey — rats, mice, shrews, rabbits.

The pawmarks of the mink on the sand — he wanted necklaces, bracelets like that.

He'd also have liked bracelets like the otter's pawmarks on the sand with webbing between five toes.

Eelgrass, after its crop in September and October, carpets the tide-edge on the black sands – like Haiti – alongside the Nun's Strand with deposits in November.

To walk on this your tackies – trainers – get slightly wet but the feeling is luxuriant.

The white-breasted black brent geese have heard of these deposits in the Canadian High Arctic and can be seen on the black sands, known as Rhenafoyle, alongside the Nun's Strand, in November, and heard calling to one another.

It was in November that Delvcaem was murdered.

Ropes hang from trees in Moyross, north Limerick city, so boys can swing from them.

Little girls play with pogo sticks.

A lemon sulky is drawn by a tittuping scarlet caparisoned, stockinged, snowy Irish draught horse, driven by a Traveller boy in Bronx 69 T-shirt, who's speaking on a mobile phone.

Another Traveller boy, in Sex Pistols T-shirt, rides a wild Arabian horse.

There's a jilted junior bicycle among the bulrushes, a discarded lady's slingback shoe with high, slender heel.

On the gateposts of one house are stone herons and in the garden of another a plastic, life-size horse.

In the garden of Delvcaem's house, the house of mourning, are scarlet mushrooms with white polka dots.

Primroses – *sabhaircíní* – are growing.

By the door a mother duck in bonnet, blue pinafore, child duck in blue apron carrying yellow roses.

Delvcaem's mother answers the door, still in her dressing gown, patterned with daisies among dill-like foliage.

Sapphire-blue eyes, cinereous mare's tail.

It is Delvcaem's nineteenth birthday.

The forget-me-not – *lus míonla* (gentle herb) – is returning to the Shannon banks.

In north Kerry they light the paschal fire on Cnoc an Óir – the hill of gold, the hill of autumn – to commemorate St Patrick, who outwitted the druids by lighting the paschal flame before the flame of Lá Bealtaine – May Day.

On Delvcaem's bedroom wall is a torso shot of Richey Edwards of Manic Street Preachers – scrolled rose tattoo on left arm – never seen since February 1995 when his Vauxhall Cavalier was found at a service station by the Severn estuary, which has the second highest tide in the world; Justin Timberlake in small-band denim cowboy hat; Shayne Ward with cobweb facial hair; Lee Otway with mouse-nest blonde hair, bone necklace, white singlet with stardust; Boy George in Welsh lady's hat; Christina Aguilera of the Marlene Dietrich mouth in mid-thigh dress of Tyrian purple and fishnet stockings; Britney Spears and troupe of dancers in Catholic girls' school uniforms; Sugababes in décolleté sequinned black; the Garryowen Pipe and Drum Band in forage caps and white gaiters; Andy Lee of Southill, Limerick city, with his opponent, Alfredo Angulo López, at the 2004 Athens Olympics; grinning teenage Kildare boxing star, David Oliver Joyce, with boxing gloves poised at the camera.

On a rack are intersport jerseys – rugby, soccer, Gaelic – from Elverys Sports shop, won from a voucher on a Coca-Cola bottle.

Delvcaem was wearing a zippie jacket with the words '*El Club que Encajona*' – the club that fits together – black-and-cream shoes with winkle-picker toes, when he was murdered.

Beaten on the head with an iron bar outside an off-licence, knife through the temple.

Nedeen, Moss, Macla, Gobby were with him when he was attacked, all on the way home from a martial arts film, *Kung Fu Hustle*, at the Omniplex.

Delvcaem ran.

Attackers pursued him.

Gobby – Gobby Kissane – shaven head, face a medley of bruises, scars and bur-marigold coloured freckles, followed and held him before the ambulance arrived.

'I'm dying,' were Delvcaem's last words.

Gobby wore a viridian soccer jacket with orange zipper, words 'The Shamrock Luck'.

Christina Aguilera had just married Jordan with a reception held over three days among cherry-blossom trees in a Californian vineyard and two months previously Sean Preston Federline had been born to Britney Spears and dancer Kevin Federline.

Delvcaem, changing hair; sometimes black, sometimes honey-blonde.

Tattoos that came on and off.

Baseball cap sideways, armlet tattoo on left arm.

Which boy was it?

Who was it?

The question mark of a forelock surviving all the hair dyes.

I rifle through the faces at Parteen swimming hole on a Saturday the previous July.

A boy with guinea-gold Titus cut by a Shannon canal with tattoo tapestry on his body like Justin Timberlake, eyes the blue of a campus of bluebells.

The salmon were so plentiful here once they used to jump into boats.

People used to row up to Sunday Mass here, once, because Parteen Church kept summer time in winter and Mass was therefore an hour later in winter.

The boy surrounded by Moyross boys with faces like the underparts of the mistle thrush from intensity of freckles.

Fiend dog on his chest, Celtic cross on his back.

His body told a story the way the Ruthwell Cross in Scotland tells the story of the 'Dream of the Rood' – the dream of the tree hewn down at the wood's edge so that Christ could be crucified on it.

Classicizing tulip-white shorts.

Incipient posture to his body, like the feet of the whooper swan

– lemon-and-ebony bill – who flourishes in the Shannon Callows (water meadows) a little to the north.

As if he was afraid of something.

But in spite of this, true to the alternative meaning of *eala*, the Irish word for swan – noble person.

Because it was a good summer the death's head hawkmoth – skull shape (eye sockets and jaws) on thorax – was sighted on a hawthorn bush.

One of the boys touched it and it issued a high-pitched squeak like a mobile phone announcing a text message is about to arrive.

The word used for penis at this swimming hole is 'langur'.

Same word as the long-tailed Asian monkey.

After the Moyross boys had gone there were pages with photographs of ladies with blow-dry hair dos administering shiny, black dildos to their rears, all over the bank.

As a child in Moyross Delvcaem would collect ladybirds in Cara – friend – matchboxes.

> Ladybird, ladybird, fly away home
> Your house is on fire, your children will burn.

At St Nessan's Community College he was later told that these words referred to the firing of hop fields in Kent after harvest.

He was also told in St Nessan's Community College about the Irish hop pickers swept away and drowned at Hartlake Bridge in Kent in 1853, a few years after the Great Famine.

He'd visited the Famine graveyard near Mitchelstown, County Cork, once with his parents when they were travelling to visit his grandmother who lived at Green's Bridge, Kilkenny town.

In St Nessan's Community College was a framed photograph of Tom Crean, Antarctic explorer from Annascaul, County Kerry, and companion of Robert Falcon Scott, in a sledge that had a flag on it with a harp in the centre.

Delvcaem was informed that Christmas Day was celebrated on 21 June in the Antarctic, and that Tom Crean had seal soup under a Christmas tree made of ski sticks, decorated with penguin feathers.

Delvcaem gave up fruit pastilles and cinder toffees – toffees that looked like ashes – for Lent.

For his Confirmation in Corpus Christi Church, Moyross, he got a white-gold neck chain from Argos.

He had a buff Airedale called Bisto who wore a scarlet dog collar with a pattern of white dog bones. Bisto's favourite food was Jonnie Onion Rings and Drifter bars.

In the summers he and his friends used to camp by Plassey Castle.

He'd go with his mother on Saturdays to admire the black-bordered blue speculum – wing colouring – of the mallard at Westfields' Bird Sanctuary, the mallard's glossy green head, purple-brown breast, and also the features of the red-breasted merganser.

He got his first detention sheet at St Nessan's Community College because he failed to bring an apple in a box to school for a science experiment.

Skinny-dipping with the Kilkenny boys in the Nore at Caney Woods when he visited his grandmother.

He once brought a bunch of field roses from the edge of Caney Woods to his grandmother.

He boxed with Garra Beasley, sheep-coloured hair in a turf cut, at St Francis' Boxing Club, where Andy Lee learned to box, near Four Star Pizza, near Lidl's German supermarket with its sign of blue, yellow and Indian red.

Garra Beasley had no pubic hair until he was fourteen, then a handsel of blonde hair.

He moved from Moyross to live in a trailer in Southill, near Limerick jail.

Delvcaem would meet him then to stand on a table against the wall at Colbert Station, put there for the purpose, to watch soccer matches in adjoining Jackman Park.

Garra now always wore a baseball hat with the colours of the French flag; blue, white with red peak.

Delvcaem got four valentines one year.

Two the next.

Only one the year after that.

He went out with a girl called Becfola who in summer was always in a flamingo miniskirt with double-serrated hem, flamingo calf boots, tank top that, in the way of All Saints, displayed a bellybutton.

The Missus, Delvcaem called her.

She was from Garryowen, by St John's Cathedral, where a boy neighbour had recently been repeatedly hit in the face with a hurley in the small hours, by a boy neighbour of Delvcaem's, and lost the sight of both eyes.

'We'll break windows, we'll break doors,' the song 'Boys of Garryown' went.

She asked him to guess what colour underwear she wore.

He guessed rightly. Pink, of course.

She asked him did he wear underwear with tongs legs like her grandfather?

He said no. He wore boxers with the signs of the zodiac on them.

He'd put a dab of aftershave on both ears before seeing her.

Had a nought-and-scissors haircut then – nought at the sides, scissors on top.

Took her to Donkey Ford's Chipper in John's Street, and Freda's Takeaway in Killeely.

Took her to McDonald's near St Francis' Boxing Club where he bought her a McFlurry ice cream.

When the loosestrife was shedding its petals onto the Shannon she told him she didn't want to go out with him anymore but stole six cans of Bulmers Cider from the house in doing this.

Garra Beasley got married at sixteen in the Church of the Holy Family in Southill.

They played Dion DiMucci's 'A Teenager in Love' at the reception in the Shamrock Hotel, Bunratty, with cake from Ivan's.

Dion DiMucci was given an old Gibson guitar when he was ten and learning Hank Williams' songs.

Garra Beasley and his wife honeymooned in Amsterdam where they found they had to be twenty-one to get into sex shops.

Delvcaem's grandmother in Kilkenny sent him fifty euros and died.

He forgot to set his watch forward, one year, and arrived at Corpus Christi Church in Moyross one hour early for Mass.

When asked what he was doing for that hour, he said he was praying.

Aelred, his cousin, in Margate, Kent, with a tattoo bulldog with the words 'Proud to be British', was killed in a quad accident at Studland beach near Bournemouth and someone sent a wreath of red roses in quad shape to the service at Long Melford Church, Suffolk.

Bobby Dazzler, he'd called Delvcaem on a visit to Limerick.

Spent his time with Mush, a Buffer – settled – Traveller friend after his dating Becfola.

'Cous' (cousin), Mush called him.

Mush – two curls like a cat's whiskers on his forehead, his hair dyed canary yellow, parted in the middle, flapper-style – had the habit of regaling compère Cilla Black of *Blind Date*, his chest bare, taking a few steps towards the television and shaking his fist at her.

Traveller boys, with diamonds or boxes hairstyles – step top, diamond- or box-pattern at the sides – would sit around afterwards drinking WKD (blue, yellow, green or red vodka), Stonehouse beer, Bavaria Crown lager, listening to music presented by DJ Tiësto, DJ Pulse, DJ Rankin, or Lisa Lashes of Tidy Trax Girls' fame, familiar to Aelred as regular DJ at Slinky's in Bournemouth.

Occasionally in the small hours Traveller boys would doff their shirts and bare-knuckle box for bets of two hundred euros.

Mush's car was torched and he moved to the cormorant coast of Galway.

Delvcaem also had a friend, Heapy, hair on the road between chestnut and nasturtium, a kick-boxer who had a tattoo 'KICK' on his buttock from a tattoo shop in Fermoy, County Cork, where Daubenton's bats hang upside down in cracks under the bridge all day, making wide circles very close to the water at dusk as they grab insects off the surface with their larger-than-usual hind feet.

Heapy joined the FCA – Local Defence Force – in Roscommon town.

The Shannon, the Shiven and the Suck were the rivers up there, glistening white with river-crowfoot blossom in summer.

Heapy would spend his time, when he wasn't training, standing around Goff Street with other young soldiers or in a pub whose sign said in Irish it was for the rakes – *réicí*.

Heapy told Delvcaem how Lieutenant Kevin Gleeson's Irish UN peacekeeping patrol was ambushed in Niemba, November 1960, by screaming tribesmen using poisoned arrows.

Lieutenant Gleeson, said Jambo, raising his left hand in a peaceful sign.

They sent an arrow through it.

Eight Irish soldiers were killed.

One died later from wounds.

There were two survivors.

A patrol under Commandant Hogan, Irish Battalion second-in-command, came across one of the two survivors, Private Thomas Kenny, with two arrows in him.

He saluted and said he was Private Kenny, Thomas.

Driven by Gobby Kissane, Delvcaem started going to north Kerry.

Gobby would do doughnuts (handbrake turns) on the sand.

Gobby always wore a woollen cap with 'Prague' on it for these trips to the Atlantic.

Casinos where men of fifty, who have children up to twenty-five, merge with boys from Limerick in camouflage baseball caps or with Traveller couples on honeymoon – youth with a tattoo of a panther with wide-open rose mouth, horseshoe penetrated by a dagger, girl with mascara blue as the kingfisher's wing and fillet orange as the kingfisher's breast.

'Have you got euro? Have you got euro?' fellow Moyross boys importuned.

A boy in the casino who looked like a heron in jeans said of Midleton, County Cork, where he was from, that it had the highest suicide rate in Ireland.

A boy in the casino, with a laugh like a kookaburra, in a hoodie jacket, told Delvcaem his parents were alcoholics and he'd take the twenty euros they gave him for food and gamble it in the casinos, buying hashish or marijuana – weed – if he won.

The bouncer had two crucifixes upside down around his neck, the smaller hanging from a crown of thorns, a miniature rifle.

'I was deported from England in 1974 for fighting for my country,' he said under Britney Spears' 'From the Bottom of My Broken Heart'.

Summers then when seven-spot ladybirds came out like stars, rag-wort grew up high as human beings, and the seagulls were your first cousins.

Bearded skewbald horses became attached to you and nearly followed the bus with Bus Éireann's logo – orange setter with legs gathered in – back to Limerick.

Snail shells of mahogany and sunflower colouring, smashed by a stone, indicated this was the anvil stone of a song thrush so he could eat the snails within.

The mistle thrush sang on a 'No Trespassers' sign and at Clancy's Strand, by meadows where nasturtiums that had run away from home lived, they threw greyhounds into the Atlantic, who could no longer run at Shelbourne Park, Dublin.

A scarecrow wore a T-shirt, 'Irish by birth, Munster by the grace of God'.

Delvcaem took a digital photograph on his mobile phone of a topaz-and-ebony she-goat, jet-black kid, two nougat-coloured kids, monarchial consort.

Hashish through horse tranquillizers to ecstasy, LSD, speed, cocaine, were used on Castle Green.

Delvcaem asked a toy boy with the features of a bottlenose dolphin in pursuit of mackerel why he had broken someone's nose.

The boy replied: 'Because I'm suffering from ADHD [Attention Deficit Hyperactivity Disorder].'

Strobe lights at the disco were like the garnet red of the burnet moth hovering over ragwort.

Delvcaem brought a girl, who looked like poultry stuffed into jeans, behind Buckley's Garage and made love to her.

Afterwards his body smelled like the urine the fox sprays to denote its territory trail.

Two stories he heard about the mink.

One, they'd been bought from Canada in the 1950s and escaped from primitive mink farms.

Two, they'd been brought from Sweden, Poland, Romania and Russia several years back and had been released by animal activists.

They were shooting mink in Galway because they raided farmyard fowl.

Old and unwanted greyhounds were flung into the Atlantic at Clancy's Strand.

Was Delvcaem victim of a ghetto kangaroo court or a tribal fight?

'If a Shankey sees a Cullivan and the Cullivan is just standing there the Shankey will go up and give him a clout.'

'Don't go over to where the Shankeys live whatever you do. You'd be found with the fishes in the morning.'

Plaster of Paris statues of Our Lady of Medjugorje were placed by a tree near the off-licence where Delvcaem was murdered.

Our Lady of Medjugorje had been appearing to a group of young adults of Delvcaem's age in the Croatian village of Medjugorje, Bosnia and Herzegovina, since June 1981, telling the visionaries that these were her final appearances on earth, and despite the subsequent war, hundreds of thousands of pilgrims were still making their way there.

Bunches of red carnations on the tree the way bunches of sea asters grow on the sea cliffs in north Kerry in autumn.

When women threw themselves off the Metal Bridge bunches of flowers would be left in the bushes at Thomondgate Dock.

Even the black Our Lady of Montserrat found her way into the tree by the off-licence.

Girls in shell-pink exercise suits, black leggings with their skirts, scarlet ankle boots, Playboy Bunny earrings, belts with Playboy Bunny buckles – diamanté bunnies with magenta eyes – silver kewpie dolls, with wine- or blue-coloured glass flowers on their pinafores, around their necks, studs in pierced cheeks, hoop earrings like Rihanna, kept vigil, carrying the flowers of autumn – Michaelmas daisies, asters, heliotrope, veronicas, clematis, knotweed.

'In Rama was there a voice heard ...'

I walk away from the house of mourning.

'JCB' by Nizlopi plays from a car stereo.

Some boys are roller-blading.

Others are having a water-balloon fight.

In good summers you see the half mourner butterfly – after the black-and-white dress worn in the period following full mourning – on the buddleia that grows in abundance by the walls here.

Bobby Dazzler ...

Delvcaem in his Confirmation jacket; Delvcaem in paisley-pattern neckerchief; Delvcaem in Ordinary Boys diamond-pattern sleeveless jersey; Delvcaem in pink-and-silver party styrofoam Stetson for his eighteenth birthday; Delvcaem with naked torso in hipster-level jeans, Le Coq Sportif boxers showing, naval-length chain, slight advertisement of pubic hair; Delvcaem with Adolf moustache; Delvcaem in space-age sunglasses and black boots with white laces; Delvcaem in Liverpool jersey with Carragher on it.

The Severn estuary has the second-highest tide in the world.

There were packets of Embassy Regal cigarettes scattered in the back seat of small-town south Wales-boy Richey Edwards' car when it was found.

The Shannon is in spring flood and at Curragower Falls boys in wetsuits, where Delvcaem is not included, brave kayaks through the tide.

Essex Skipper

Traveller's joy on the hedges becomes old man's beard in the autumn.

When I was a boy my father gave me a collection of art books, loose reproductions going with them.

One of the reproductions was *The Drunkenness of Noah* by Michelangelo – a naked, wreathed youth, whose own genitals are showing, covering the nakedness of Noah who has a wine jug alongside him, the youth's head turned back to a naked young man who is gloating over Noah's embarrassment.

Men known as breeches-makers were employed by the Vatican, I tell the two boys who are visiting me – one of whom looks like a Cyclops or a myopic pine marten – to cover the nakedness of Michelangelo youths – *ignudi* – with ribbons, drapery, entire garments.

But this one escaped.

I tell them the story as they look at the painting:

As an old man Michelangelo was walking through the snow to the Coliseum when Cardinal Farnese accosted him and asked him why a man of his age was out in the snow.

'To learn something new,' was the famous reply.

Giovanni Bellini, from whose mastery of light the hour of the day can be deduced, gave a version of old age in those loose reproductions: Noah with beard of ermine and baby-nakedness.

The boys also look at Mary Cassatt's *Mother and Child*: naked American he-child who looks as if he's destined for a career in the navy.

Mary Cassatt took her influence from Correggio, I tell the boys.

In Chapter 14 of Mark, Christ is deserted by all except a boy wearing nothing but a linen cloth who follows Him as He's being taken away, gives Him the cloth and runs away naked.

Correggio painted this scene but the painting is lost.

There's a copy of it in Parma; boy with vermilion cloak on his shoulder being pursued by a soldier in an indigo cuirass.

The following Monday the guards investigate.

A young detective in black jobber – half-boots – pays attention to *The Rape of Ganymede*, thought to have been by Titian, by Damiano Mazza, in which the rapist eagle has a decurved beak and wings with ctenoid edges – like the teeth of a comb, Ganymede's buttocks resolved for penetration while coral-pink drapery liberates itself from his body.

François Boucher's *Cupid* with his love arrows in a gold-topped scarlet pouch is examined.

Even a child with golden hair and painted cheeks in biscuit (marble-like) unglazed porcelain by the eighteenth-century Düsseldorf sculptor Johann Peter Melchior is scrutinized.

Sent by the girlfriend of a boy dying of Aids, I'd thought it for many years to have been a depiction of Melchior, one of the three wise men, his name meaning king of light.

An older detective seems unsettled by Franz von Lebach's *The Little Shepherd*: boy in scarlet waistcoat, short trousers like the ones Hugo von Hofmannsthal wore in his prodigious Viennese boyhood, lying among poppies.

The young detective picks up the Penguin edition of Alain-Fournier's *Le Grand Meaulnes* with a black-and-white photograph of a boy's naked torso on the cover, an *ignudo* shadowed by leaves.

Certain evidence of paedophilia and he consults with the clerkish older detective.

I had a copy of this book as a child with Sisley's *Small Meadows in Spring* on the cover ... black-stockinged girl by poplars ... blue

ribbon around her hat ... head dipped as if she's admiring a flower
in her hand ... Augustin Meaulnes used to gather the eggs of the
red-headed moorhen in meadows such as these for his mother.

The great black-backed gull eats other gulls.

Earlier I was arrested on the strand by the young detective.

A file of five guards or detectives came into my chalet like
Spanish inquisitors in their cone hats.

A stout, rugby-playing ban garda (woman garda) looks through my
album with images from the Národní Gallery in Prague, the State
Gallery in Stuttgart, collections in Arnhem, Cracow.

My shoes are confiscated and I am put in a cell with a ground
latrine and the name Dinny scrawled on the wall.

Mudlarks with bumfluff moustaches and German shepherd dogs
alongside them search for golf balls in the shallow river of this town.

I am interrogated under video camera.

I make no comments.

On my return to my chalet, despite the fact I'm next door to
the garda station, I find the two windows broken.

A gang of boys approach the chalet four times, completely
demolishing the back-lane window glass so people can climb through.

A heavy rock is thrown in at me.

'Come out here. But call the ambulance first.'

'That was only a crowd of young lads who did that,' a young
ginger-haired guard, who arrives on the scene, tells me.

After four nights of terror I abandon the chalet in haste.

The curtains of the bedroom I move into in Tralee have been rubbed
with faeces.

A drunken youth tries to break into my room one night, accus-
ing me of stealing a Radiohead CD.

One of the house residents served with Global Strategy Mercenaries in Iraq, saw the North Gate of Baghdad, and when I try to

ask him about his experiences he threatens me with the IRA.

'What do you want to know about that for?'

I stayed in the Salvation Army hostel in Edinburgh once and this is just like it.

There was a former professor from St Andrews University who'd made the hostel his home.

I swim near a lighthouse.

The ringed plover – *feadóg an fháinne* – lives in abundance here.

When threatened it drags its body along the ground, tail spread, one wing extended and flapping as if it was injured.

I recognize the black armpits of the grey plover – *feadóg ghlas* – which you can see in flight.

I move into a tiny room near the Lee River that flows into Trá Lí Mic Dedad (the beach of Lí, son of Dedad).

I frequently spot a heron by the river.

Cinder-sifter boys search for discarded carbonators by this river, which can be used for plumbing or heating.

Girls sit on the crossbars of boys' bicycles like visiting aristocracy in the howdah on an elephant's back.

'I thought someone just left it here,' a boy tells me as I stop him stealing my bicycle.

A crowd of school children bang on my back-lane window.

I look out.

'Queer,' one calls back.

A few evenings later, a Friday evening, there is a knock on the window.

It is the same boy. A tall gander-like boy. An adolescent gorilla.

His T-shirt says: 'I'm a workaholic. Every time I work I need a beer.'

He asks if he can come in.

'I want to stay the night with you,' he says.

I bring him to the beach and give him my spare swimming briefs, which he jogs in while I swim.

In a corner of the beach he towels himself naked.

Gooseberry-velutinous chest – soft, fine hairs; moustachial hairs under his navel; genitals the salmon red of the linnet's breast.

The geography of Essex with its many tidal rivers in its early body hair.

He is the young warrior who, after letting his beloved hawk fly into the Weald, advances towards his doom in battle with the Vikings as the causeway tide goes out.

Bricin – Bricin Pluckrose is his name.

His father is from the wastes of Essex near Chelmsford.

Bricin brings a childhood snapshot of himself in rag hat with butterfly on it – Essex skipper, orange with black rim.

He brings a photograph of his father standing against a Union Jack in olive-green polo shirt with red-rimmed collar, black braces, black laced-up boots.

His father used to sell fruit and vegetables in Chelmsford in scarlet work boots with white laces, jeans with rolled-up ends, scarlet braces and shaven head like William Pitt's niece and social hostess Lady Hester Stanhope, who used to beat her servants in Phoenicia with a mace and employed an ex-general of Napoleon as soothsayer there.

His father's sister – his nan – was a skinhead.

'No earring but a bald head. No jail record.'

She said then: 'I want to slow down and marry.'

She married a heavyweight boxer in Brentwood.

'He saved my bacon,' she said of him.

The boy who tells these stories has hair the black of the defensive liquid the ten-armed cuttlefish emits, pockmarks like the webbing between the sea otter's feet, Rudolph Valentino in mayhem good looks, mackerel-blue eyes.

Eyes that suddenly liquify into anguish at the remembrance of some insult or some uncertainty as to my expectations of him.

They are different expectations, new expectations.

Occasionally his eyes rivet dangerously.

Speech is frequently interrupted; a stammer, a caesura.

The Queen's father, George VI, had a stammer, I tell him.

His grandmother, who witnessed the Canvey Island disaster of February 1953, has a framed message from George VI on her incrusted line-patterned wallpaper.

'Help to make the world a better place and life a worthier thing.'

'She's with the fairies,' Bricin borrows an expression from his Irish mother who drinks an eggnog every night and occasionally a Club Dry Gin with it.

Bricin disappears from my life just as the Essex skipper vanishes from a musk thistle.

> She is the fairies' midwife ...
> Her waggon-spokes made of long spinners' legs;
> The cover, of the wings of grasshoppers ...
> Her chariot is an empty hazel-nut ...

It is St Patrick's night and the shelter from which I swim is invaded.

A bin filled with glass from occasional winter drinkers has been emptied out.

A small English boy with a café-crème baseball cap and a jail-bird stride indicates he carries a flick knife.

A girl in a T-shirt with the words 'Oopsy Tipsy! One too Many' is walking around with jeans down to her knees.

A flamingo bottom like François Boucher's toiletting Venus.

In the Boucher painting putti-bearing chaplets administer to Venus.

Here the putti wear baseball caps.

I ask two of these putti – one with a T-shirt with the words: 'So wotcha say?' – to look after my bicycle while I'm swimming.

They throw it to the ground, smashing the lamp to smithereens.

A girl with 'Will try anything twice' flaunted on her T-shirt throws grit at me as I change.

I ask her to stop whereupon the putti who threw my bicycle to the ground approach to beat me up.

I manage to appease them and I make a getaway from this demonic theatre.

A boy with Fatty Arbuckle features, hair and freckle colouring of the red squirrel, eyes blue as hedge periwinkles, in tropical shirt and Dr Livingstone shorts reconciles me to Bricin.

He delivers him to me.

The following Friday as he eats a forest-berry Bavarian cream cake he tells me that his cousin Uinseann – Gaelic for Vincent – who has Adam Ant braids, eyes like the Japanese sika deer in Killarney National Park, and tennis-star sisters Venus and Serena Williams on his mobile phone, used to make love to him in the shower of his home.

Bricin is wearing a J. Nistlerooy, Manchester United, black away shirt.

Uinseann has a girlfriend now who has beet-red dye in her hair, wears Mickey Mouse knickers, and said to Bricin: 'If you were a product you'd be mustard.'

They went to a nightclub in Tralee together where the boys danced with the boys and the girls danced with the girls and a boy and a girl had oral sex on the floor.

When Bricin is distressed he can make his jaws look like the Aristotle's lantern – the spherical jaws of a sea urchin.

Alternatively, he diverts to his father's Essex Polari – a mixture of pig Latin, Romany, criminal argot.

Dosh, he calls money.

In the casinos, some boys sell themselves for sex for twenty euros.

My father, donor of Michelangelos and Bellinis – from the books he gave me I learnt that Leonardo wrote in mirror writing (reversed writing) – referred to my girlfriends as Mary Annes.

Also known as Mary Annes were the London telegraph boys of the 1880s in their light-blue uniforms and sideways caps, whom speculation said satisfied the desires of the heir presumptive with spiv's moustache and frogged Hussar's tunic, who, on his early death, was mourned each day by his mother, with fresh flowers laid on his deathbed.

One of those London Mary Annes was found to have connections with the Golden Lane Boy Brothel near the Liffey in Dublin, frequented by Dublin Fusiliers and Grenadier Guards, which the Home Rulers used as propaganda against the British rulers.

Sometimes Bricin comes into my place from the casinos like a ruffled young barn owl with its kitten head and protuberant eyes.

A man in a denim cowboy hat in the casino told him: 'I put ads in the paper and get couples. I only go with couples.'

His mouth is smeared with the Mississippi mud pie he's been eating.

Dalta – foster-child; Bricin in my life.

Late August he visits Essex with his father.

'I love this country,' his father declares when the Tube reaches Epping.

'In my childhood a mug cost a penny and very big ones too.'

They feast on jumbo sausages, curry, chips and gravy, and Memory Lane Madeira cake in Colchester.

This is a conversation Bricin hears on a bus in Colchester:

'And the cat got into the fridge.'

'How did the cat get into the fridge?'

'Don't ask me. And it was so smelly.'

In a supermarket he witnesses a youth, accosted by store detectives, pulling down his trousers in front of the delicatessen, showing his Ginch Gonch underwear.

'I haven't got anything!'

His family knows the Roman roads of Essex, the ploughman's spikenard, same fragrance as the ointment Mary anointed the feet of Jesus with.

'Goodbye Bud,' his uncle, who wears a silver lurex shirt and who has a bull terrier called Daniela, says to him when he's leaving.

He has returned from Essex wearing a black-and-white baseball cap with rabbit ears and a belt with a monkey motif buckle – three monkey cameos.

There are male strippers in Galway, Bricin has heard. For hen parties; some of them appear in nothing but Stetsons from Euro-Saver shops.

Perhaps he'll go there, wear Union Jack kit, bill himself as the Essex stripper or British kit stripper.

In September he turns up in the shelter in the evenings while I'm swimming, as a black-headed gull — chocolate-brown head — drawn to sportsfields, does.

Body like a wounded gull.

Joins hands, prays for his dead Irish grandfather.

'If he was alive he'd give me fifty euros.'

Often he lights candles in church for his grandfather before coming to meet me.

Here he may spend a votive ten minutes.

His mother got a portrait tattoo of his grandfather in Limerick on her right arm.

His grandfather used to wear a hat with a scarlet cockade and pheasant feather on the brim.

I have to ban Bricin from my place. Coming too often, danger.

He bangs on my window for admittance, like the busty Caroline of Brunswick, in spite of her affair with Italian courtier Bartolomeo Pergami, banging on the doors of Westminster Abbey during the coronation of her husband George IV, the doors barred against her.

The Polish boy who fixes my bicycle is from Katowice, Henryk Górecki's town, composer of *Symphony of Sorrowful Songs*, a tape lost in my flight.

The bicycle man with handlebar moustache frequently passes me in a Toyota truck and honks at me.

I arrived on the first of November, a Friday — Samhain — to have my bicycle chain fixed.

He was in jail for not paying his taxes, an old lady, who reprimanded me for wearing shorts in November, told me.

I called at the buff bungalow of a boy, who wore a lemon

baseball cap with the words 'The Doctor', who'd pledged to help me if I was in trouble with my bicycle.

He ambushed a girl with tricolour hair – hazel in front, fuschia on top, ebony ponytail – on a madder rose junior bicycle, which featured the bobbed-haired Dora the Explorer in lemon ankle socks, and forcibly took a link from her chain.

She threatened the Demon Man on him.

The link didn't fit.

I was led to a greensward where boys in a flea market of baseball caps stood around a Samhain bonfire.

Between the first of November and the first of May the *filí* – poets – would tell a story for each night.

A Raleigh racing bicycle, which wobbled like jelly, was produced from a shed.

I was asked twenty-five euros for it.

I only had twenty-two euros.

I was given it for that and I walked the two bicycles the ten miles back against the night traffic and met a man with greyhounds, pink and white electric-fence twine attached to them.

The hermit crab crawls into the mollusc abandoned by the mussel or the oyster.

A nosegay of snowdrops – *pluiríní sneachta* – comes to my door.

A child is a graph; he measures the year.

I see him again in a scarlet-and-navy-banded blue-striped Tommy Hilfiger jersey and pointy shoes, eyes the blue of the hyacinths the rubbish-dump-frequenting herring gull decorates its nest with; white polo shirt with vertically blue-striped torso, listening to Rihanna's 'Good Girl Gone Bad' on his mobile phone; I see him crunching a Malteser – small round chocolate with honeycombed centre – sucking a strawberry Fun Gum or biting on a raspberry and pineapple Fruit Salad bar; I see his eyes again, blue as the blue pimpernel flower of Essex.

There was a honey-haired and honey-browed young drug dealer who ultimately used to reside in the shelter in the evenings.

His mother's people were from The Island in Limerick, where swans colonize the turloughs (winter lakes) with a view of council houses beyond.

On his motorbike, with yellow backpack, he'd travel over rivers like the Oolagh and the Allaghaun, to places like Rooskagh, to sell marijuana and hashish to boys waiting on summer evenings in dia-mond-pattern shorts.

The Lueneburg Manuscript of the middle of the fifteenth century tells how in the year 1284, on the twenty-sixth of June, Feast of Saints John and Paul, one hundred and thirty children from Hamelin, Ger-many, were led from the town by a piper dressed in diverse colours to a place of execution behind the hills. A stained-glass window in Mark-tkirche, Hamelin, depicted the colours. Jacob Ludwig Carl and William Carl Grimm, known to embellish, retold the story.

Were the children drowned in the Weser?

Did they depart on a Children's Crusade?

Were they murdered in the forest by the piper?

Did they anticipate Theresienstadt where children were allowed to paint in diverse colours before being gassed?

Did they anticipate the children pulled out from the rubble in Dresden, on a night a Vermeer was burned, in Harlequin and Pierrot costumes because the bombing of Dresden took place at Fasching – Shrovetide carnival?

Divers colours: the paintings of Michelangelo, Leonardo, Gio-vanni Bellini, Damiano Mazza – two boys look at them and then, like the two children of Hamelin who didn't follow the piper, debouch to the garda station to report this montage of pornography.

Old Swords

Luke Wadding, seventeenth-century Waterford friar in Rome, who sent the sword of the Earl of Tyrone – buried in the Franciscan Convent of San Pietro in Montorio – back to Cromwellian-overrun Ireland, did most of his writing between sunset and midnight, we were told at National School …

On her fern- and ivy-collecting visit to County Kerry in the late summer of 1861, shortly before her husband's death from shock over his son's affair with an actress, Queen Victoria was presented with a davenport writing desk, lions and unicorns rampant on it, made by three Killarney carpenters, the surviving brother of the Liberator Daniel O'Connell coming to meet her in the home of the Herberts, who were catapulted into bankruptcy by the expenses Queen Victoria incurred for them.

The stories come back like the lesser celandine blossoms by the sea in early spring: stories from history, stories from your life …

The parents of Iarla Corduff, whose hair was the pale red-bronze of the grouse when affiliated to heather, eyes the green of the County Clare Burren moth, were married in Baltimore, Maryland, where they were emigrants.

Iarla's father worked as a fisherman and his mother was pregnant when they were summoned to the church hurriedly. Iarla's father wore his fisherman's wellingtons at the wedding.

The grouping for photographs taken at a reception at which the reel 'Salute to Baltimore' was played on an Excelsior accordion – but not any of the photographs Iarla's mother subsequently framed on the parlour flock wallpaper – wallpaper with pattern made by powdered wool: a beaming lady with clubbed hair and roll fringe, in zebra-stripe dress, holding out a tender yellow-and-faded-scarlet rectangular box of Kodak film.

Back in a *breac-ghaeltacht* – mixed Irish- and English-speaking district – she had a miscarriage picking seaweed.

Herrings between July and February, mackerel between April and July. New potatoes after July, basil near the carrots in summer, turnips September–October, the pig killed in autumn, winter cabbage, a knife on the cement for the goose near Christmas.

A finger was put to the back of the goose when it was killed so the blood went to the neck. After six hours in water the feathers fell off.

Women bathed their feet in the water corpses had been washed in because they thought it was holy water.

Uisce coisricthe.

In the parlour of their bungalow on a *tóchar* – causeway – was a picture of *The Irish Brigade before Battle* – their ancient tricolour sent back from France to the new Irish Free State and blessed anew by Father Pigott on St Patrick's Day in Cork.

The ruin of Daniel O'Connell's parents' house was near, though he himself was born in an emergency in a neighbour's cottage.

They'd kept a print of the Pretender James III there. When wives were sought for him in Europe, one was rejected because she was a dwarf.

O'Connell was fostered to his uncle Hunting Cap, who made a fortune smuggling silks and brandy.

He sent O'Connell's cousins to France to join the Irish Brigade and O'Connell himself to France to study Condillac and Helvétius, where François Boucher had shortly before painted John the Baptist in a Turkish delight-red cloak as if he'd got a loan or endowment from a king and Marie Antoinette had requested Philip Astley and his son John – the English rose – to bring the circus that Philip had introduced to England at Halfpenny Hatch, Lambeth Fields in 1768, to France.

Iarla's family had a book in their parlour beside the Pye wireless with the name Athlone on it, about O'Connell, published in Ave Maria Lane, London.

O'Connell with hair en brosse in front beside the stream where his father used to put out salt pans – vessels for getting salt by evaporation.

Iarla's mother had lovely American clothes when he was a child.

Her proudest possession a paisley shawl, the kind Pier Angeli wore, victim of a broken engagement to Kirk Douglas.

But one night she came upon two battling rats in her room and they turned on her.

She defended herself with a lighted candle and her clothes horse went on fire, her American clothes, including her paisley shawl.

However, a Charlie Chaplin brooch from Baltimore survived, which was appropriate as Charlie Chaplin, his wife Oona O'Neill and their *passeggiata* of children frequently holidayed in the area.

Ties of maple red, ties the red of a bull's rosette, ties the red of the red grouse's wattle, ties the red of the chough's legs – Iarla wore these as a child for occasions like Confirmation – *faoi láimh easpaig* (under the Bishop's hand) – Morning of the Assumption.

The National School teacher would keep a heavy girl, who excelled at making diamond-pattern bed covers, behind in the afternoons to feel inside her skirt.

She'd tell her parents she'd been kept behind for misbehaviour and they'd beat her.

In the town, under a red sandstone mountain called the Giant's Arse because it was shaped like buttocks, was a butcher, Mr O'Muirgheasa, who marched by himself down the street with a red flag every May Day.

He'd met and conversed with General de Gaulle when he'd visited the town.

Mr O'Muirgheasa claimed he'd never gone to Mass since he was a child, when the County Mayo librarian, Letitia Dunbar-Harrison, was boycotted because she was a Protestant.

Despite his irreligiosity there was a statue in his butcher shop; no one could make out whether it was Mary or a figure from Celtic mythology: a woman in white tunic, blue veil, a severed male hand on her left shoulder.

A leatherback turtle had crawled up the main street as far as the azure Player's Please sign the year Dr Gilmartin, Archbishop of Tuam, had congratulated the County Mayo commissioners responsible for the boycott of Miss Dunbar-Harrison.

Iarla shared a room with his brother, Brecan, a year older than him.

Over Iarla's bed was a colour photograph of Kirk Douglas showing his legs to Tony Curtis in *The Vikings*.

With Brecan he'd walk to the grave of Scota – daughter of the Pharaoh of Egypt, wife of Miliseus of Spain, killed at the Battle of Slieve Mis.

From there they could see Banna Strand where Sir Roger Casement landed in a German U-boat, Easter 1916, and was marched by the English to Tralee where the Royal Irish Constabulary man's wife cooked him a steak.

Casement left his pocket watch as appreciation before being moved on to his execution in Pentonville Prison.

The story, told by a Christian Brother catechism examiner, who'd felt Iarla's neonate ginger-auburn hair inside his swain's short trousers, was recorded in an exercise book with fleurons on the cover.

It was Brecan, who had a haircut like Brian Poole of the Tremeloes, who'd returned to his family's butcher business, who'd first made love to him.

Brecan slept in the Kerry colours – green and dust-gold.

There was an amorist in town, originally from Dublin, with a horse-shoe beard like Yul Brynner in *Solomon and Sheba*, who swam in winter and won best actor award at the amateur drama finals in Scarriff, County Clare.

The adjudicator at Scarriff later drove his car off Corrib Bridge by Fisheries' Field in Galway and drowned.

St Swithin of Winchester requested to be buried in the cathedral yard so his grave would be rained on, and St Swithin's Day, 15 July, determined the weather, rain or shine, for the next forty days.

It was on St Swithin's Day the Dublin man seduced Iarla in a copse behind a flank of mountain ashes after Iarla had swum in a stream.

Looking at Iarla standing naked in the stream one day, the man said he reminded him of Tom, the dirty little chimney sweep in Charles Kingsley's *The Water-Babies*, who came down his friend Ellie's chimney uninvited and subsequently, like the boys in Henry Scott Tuke's paintings, had to purify himself – Tom, the dirty little chimney sweep, immediately put on the Vatican's *Index Librorum Prohibitorum*.

Iarla was by his side in a hotel in a neighbouring town after a performance one night.

On the wall was a colour photograph of the Rose Garden, Bangor, County Down.

A taciturn-faced boy with Fräulein-blonde facial hair, eyes chestnut-fringed, green rugby player's chest, in a V-neck vermilion jersey, sat on the floor.

There was a feeling of expectancy. Was someone going to sing a song?

And then indeed the boy in the vermilion jersey did sing a song:

> I sold my rock
> I sold my reel
> When my flax was gone
> I sold my wheel
> To buy my love a sword of steel.

In the town, the drama group would meet in an Augustan pub called The White Causeway, a sign without that featured an undertaker celebrating with a glass of wine and a picture within of a bottle of wine beside a wine glass, with the words: 'Salina Helena, Napa Valley Reserve, 1917'.

The grey seals were born in autumn as white-coated pups on the Góilín – inlet – a coral strand made up of calcerous algae washed in by the winter tides.

They remained on the strand for three weeks, after which the mothers abandoned them and hunger forced them to sea.

'Most people say you're turning into a right old poufter. Other people say you're sound,' a youth in a whipcord jacket and goffered shirt said to Iarla at a dance one night when Big Tom and the Mainliners were playing.

When a poster for a parish-hall showing of *The Swordsman of Siena* – Stewart Granger in full Sienese garb waving a sword, a trembling décolleté Sylva Koscina with droplet earrings and a fearless Christine Kaufmann in a tam by his side – turned up in town, Iarla went to study in Dublin, dancing on Saturday nights in an Aran cardigan with wooden buttons at The Television Club.

He had his tarot read by a girl who sat beside him on a chaise longue in South King Street.

He threw up his studies after a year and a half and went off to England.

'The swan would die of pride if it hadn't black feet,' his mother said to him.

Her Pier Angeli had died of a barbiturates overdose.

In London he lived on pans of onions, which he fried wearing a sheepskin coat, and drank tea from a mug with Gainsborough's shepherd girl on it.

He regularly went to a pub near St Martin-in-the-Fields to hear a woman from the Donegal gaeltacht, her photograph in an Abbey Theatre programme once, recite poems she never wrote down, her bedsit in Tufnell Park a legend of cats.

She'd upbraided George Bernard Shaw when he was considering her for a major part and subsequently descended to menial work.

The death of one of her dogs in a street accident occasioned a nervous breakdown.

Iarla heard her tell an audience of Irish boys in cloaks, green-and-red half boots, Irish girls in Queen Nefertiti or Queen Nitocris shift dresses, that her poems were millions of years old.

Old as Queen Scota maybe.

A line from one of her poems about walking holding someone's hand in Ireland decided him to return to Kerry.

In early spring, by the stream, he saw again the hart's tongue fern and the lords and ladies fern and the buttercup leaves and the celandine leaves and later the hemlock and the ramsons – the wild garlic – and the alexanders and the eyebright and the goosegrass and the chickweed.

There is a red rim to the chickweed flower and he often saw that red in the whites of his eyes. It wasn't that he cried. But he was always near tears.

Near a *ráth* – an earthen ring fort – he found the small feathers of a singing thrush, which told him that a merlin had plucked its prey here, and he thought of the punitive, sometimes Augean places he'd lived in London, Thin Lizzy's album *Shades of a Blue Orphanage* borne to each of them.

Brecan managed the local Spar supermarket now, which had advertisements for Ardfert Retreat Centre.

He married a Galway girl, his mother wearing a toque of lopped coins with a cobweb veil hanging from it for the wedding, pancake make-up on her face and angel-hair eyelashes like Joan Collins' in *Esther and the King*.

After a few years in Kerry, working around the bungalow, walking to the Góilín on days when the sky looked as if it was going to kick a ball at you, time of the cuckoo's sostenuto, Iarla went to New York.

'Slán go fóill [goodbye for the moment],' said his lover friend of early adolescence, 'I hope New York does you justice.'

In Tralee before getting the bus for the onward journey he saw the Christian Brother catechism examiner of childhood hanging around the lavatory in Bill Booley's Lane.

'I went to Carthage where I found myself in the midst of a hissing cauldron of lust.'

His friend would quote St Augustine to describe a sojourn in North Africa. 'All naked boys had to wear the horn of a gazelle when they reached puberty.'

In a steam room in New York a young black soldier with a silver-dollar crew cut said: 'Balls are the nature of man. When they're big, man's nature is big. Yours are big as an infant's head.'

He worked in Irish bars in New York, mostly one on the East River whose owner was from Cois Fharraige (beside the south Connemara Atlantic).

'At sixteen I lived on the Holloway Road with just Gaelic.

'Up at six. On the road for an hour.

'We had to get it ready for the chippies. They did the slabbing and we put the plaster on it.

'One hour getting back.

'Then to the pubs.

'Madison and Fifth Avenue was a two-way system when I arrived, with gold traffic signals with small statues of Mercury, messenger of the gods, on them.

'We knew nothing about sex in Connemara.

'The priest called the shots.

'On South Boston men's beach, in a sauna, the peanut whistle going outside, we found out.'

Iarla had had a young lover friend in Dublin who was an electrician from Athlone where groups of boys hang out on the Shannon Bridge near the redstone, green-panelled Dillon Shoes building.

There were fathers in the Athlone area, that boy had told Iarla, who let their friends make love to their teenage sons and watched while they were doing it.

With a Sagittarius stone – turquoise – this boy had gone to live in Berlin.

After a year in New York, Iarla went to Toronto, Canada, country of Leonard Cohen whom he heard singing 'Kevin Barry' in a 1960s *Weltanschauung* version at a concert in Dublin.

'Just a lad of eighteen summers ...'

He lived in a house with shiplap siding in a run-down district.

There were stories about gay people thrown at night into Toronto harbour.

Occasionally he saw the Italian word *froci* – queers – written on the walls.

He sent his Dublin friend a postcard of Vuillard's *Toulouse-Lautrec* – mushroom hat, poppy shirt, baggy lemon trousers.

'Are you in the land of the living?'

The reply was an ancient John Hinde colour postcard of the town under the Giant's Arse mountain.

Shortly after Iarla got this card his mother died of cancer in Marymount Hospice in Cork, with a Norah Lofts book by her bed.

In Kerry he found her love letters to his father in a yellow, royal-blue and scarlet Weetabix cereal tin she'd sent away for with coupons she'd collected.

'I looked after old people for a penny a day when I was a girl,' she'd told Iarla once, 'put turf and bog gale under their beds.'

Iarla left Toronto shortly after returning from Kerry and went back to New York, to pubs run by Irishmen with TV-cop moustaches.

Early one winter, thrush in the mouth turned into pneumonia and he spent a winter in bed.

He thought about his friend in Berlin and then a card drifted through from him, belatedly condoling him on his mother's death: Jerg Ratgeb's *Crucifixion*; the tongue of the thief on Christ's right side hanging out, a woman in shrimp-pink gown thrusting herself at the foot of the Cross and crows pecking around the Cross in oblivion.

Big Tom and the Mainliners played in New York, attracting an audience of heroin addicts by mistake because mainlining is an American term for injecting into the main vein, and Iarla returned to Ireland for a short sojourn, going via London.

The Irish streets in London didn't seem changed; the posters in the windows, the names of singers with what were either the titles of their songs or maxims, after their names.

Dominic Kirwin: 'Always'. Sean O'Farrell: 'Today'. Joe Dolan: 'Come Early'.

An omnipresent poster: 'Brendan Shine Live'.

A black woman stood at a bus stop in embroidered lapis-lazuli garb, in blue headdress, series of filigree pendants in her ears. On the bus was the ubiquitous Irish story:

'Do you know "The Lonely Woods of Upton?" You don't know it,' the man was looking at Iarla's black leather matador jacket, 'because you've never been there.

'My mother and father didn't care about me. They gave me to an orphanage there in Ireland when I was three. She's married to another man in Scotland now. He's dead.

'I have three bairns in Scotland. People don't know how hard it is. I've got to come here and support them. And I drink. I'm nobody's child. You're nobody's child but your own.'

And then he started singing:

> Those men who died for Ireland
> In the lonely woods of Upton for Sinn Féin.

Iarla could see the contrast between the Irish in England, his London years, and New York. He'd that experience in his life, that vicissitude.

In the Postcard Gallery on Neal Street he bought a card for his Dublin friend who'd returned to his city: Alfred Eisenstaedt's *Dutch Woman and Boy Looking At Rembrandt's Nightwatchmen*, the woman with a mole on her face, shadows filling the eyes and the curious, serious mouth of the boy, her grandson, the woman's right hand clenched in threads of light.

A barred feather, which fell in his path in Kerry, told him that a sparrowhawk was close by, seeking prey.

Glebe, this place was called – earth.

A ruined castle reminded Iarla that County Kerry was known as the Kingdom.

In the small park in the town, a man in his Sunday suit played 'A Nation Once Again' on bagpipes under a statue of Kerry Antarctic explorer Tom Crean with ski sticks – who'd been seen off on one of his voyages by the Dowager Empress Marie Feodorovna, mother of Tzar Nicholas II, who, with his wife Princess Alix of Hesse, Queen Victoria's granddaughter, and his children, was murdered in a blood-stained cellar in Ekaterinburg in 1918 – two women with reticules seated on a stone bench watching the performance, the older with pumps with almond-shaped toes, the younger with French pleat at the back of her hair.

A Denny van drew up during the recital, with four lonely-looking sausages on the van.

Iarla thought his experience of the west of Ireland was the experience of a missing face, like the face of a boy, chestnut-fringed green eyes, in a V-neck vermilion jersey, he'd seen at a party in a hotel after a play once, a woman belting out Isabel Leslie's 'The Thorn Tree' that night as she played on a piano with a red silk front.

'But if your heart's an Irish heart you'll never fear the thorn tree.'

The green-headed mallard, who mates with our farmyard geese, stays for summer, but I must go.

Before flying back to New York, where he found the helper, suppressor cells were quickly vanishing from his body, Iarla met a man with a turf cut, in suede shoes with a metallic sheen, above Clancy's Strand in Limerick.

'You wouldn't think I'd want to have my hair short,' he said, 'I was in the army for so long. I was out in the Lebanon. I saw a man choke his own daughter. She was handicapped and showed her panties. You wouldn't think I'd miss the Lebanon. But I do.'

'Old friends, like old swords, still are trusted best ...'

Iarla's friend told him about his own swim and the winter swim in Dublin; of the chute at Blackrock Baths; of bathing places with graffiti urging assignations; of jetties into the Irish Sea, which people wandered as if seeking revelations; of two villas called Milano and La Scala adjacent to the sea near his home; of going to *Song of Norway* performed at a theatre with organ-pipe pillars on either side of the stage – the women in dirndls (Alpine costumes); of an attempt at being a seminarist; then the profligacy of men's swimming places – cormorants flying low over the gnashing and discontented sea at swimming coves, academic-looking seals coursing by you while in England a peer sent to jail for alleged sexual assault on two Boy Scouts in a beach hut and the police raiding men's houses and examining their photograph albums; of bran-faced young FCA men fresh from army summers at Finner Camp offering themselves for fellation at urinals with the word 'FIR' (men) outside, the experience of serving in the Belgian Congo where gonorrhoea being rampant greatly increased the numbers of soldiers in urinals; of the ship that brought him past the swimming places of Dublin Bay, the cerulean mountains that virtually formed letters of the alphabet, the nimbused valleys, to the minarets of North Africa; of how earlier in the century Mr Carson approached the Forty Foot in winter with a lantern, would swim to Bullock Harbour in Dalkey and back, was prosecuted and fined two and sixpence for swimming naked in 1906; of Dr Oliver St John Gogarty who was taken captive during the Civil War in January 1923 by men who entered his house using a woman, later to become a nun in Rathmines, as a decoy, was taken to a house near Salmon Pool on Island Bridge to be shot, twice claimed he had to urinate outside because of nervousness, second time threw himself into the Liffey and swam, was swept along by the current, came to a house where he was given brandy by a garda doctor. In 1924 he presented two swans, which were sent from Lady Leconfield's lake in Sussex, to the goddess of the Liffey as thanksgiving. The swans wouldn't get out of the crate so W.B. Yeats, who was presiding over the ceremony, had to give the crate a good kick.

Cicero — as the pupils of Green's CBS in Tralee in their blue-grey jerseys know — told the story:

The young courtier Damocles in the city of Syracuse was heard to envy his lord Dionysius whereupon Dionysius proposed he sit on his throne for one day and the feasting Damocles noticed a sharp sword hanging over him by a thread, the price of power!

Iarla had Richard Westall's paintings from the Postcard Gallery, Neal Street, London — a Neronic young man not unlike the neoclassical rugby youths in the showers of O'Dowd Park, Tralee.

Wasn't there the story too, passed down from a drama adjudicator who'd drowned himself, of Georges d'Anthe, white horseguards' uniform, wavy blonde hair — perhaps like the youth in the hotel — the adopted son of the Dutch ambassador of St Petersburg and reputedly his pathic, who fell in love with Alexander Pushkin's wife, a 'Raphael hour', and slew Pushkin, whose winter coat was missing a button, in a duel?

In the National Portrait Gallery in London, Iarla had seen the portrait of Robert Devereux, Second Earl of Essex, after Marcus Gheeraerts the Younger, with chin-frizz beard, whose face Elizabeth I had slapped after he'd turned his back on her.

In Essex Birhtnoth's beautiful and ornamented sword was coveted and Birhtnoth slain by the causeway — *tóchar*.

> Then would he wish to see my Sword, and feel
> The quickness of the edge, and in his hand
> Weigh it ...

Perhaps he picked up the HIV virus from a youth from Red Wing, Missouri, with a Joe Dallesandro headband.

There'd been a priest, a Raphael hour, eyes the blue of the chicory that grew at the béguinage gates at home, he'd made love to in an apartment full of street jewellery in New York, he wasn't sure of.

Between waking and sleeping in a Brooklyn hospital, after listening to a broadcast of Jessye Norman singing in Central Park to commemorate Princess Diana, Iarla dreams of Dr Oliver St John Gogarty, a story from his adolescence, a fellow Irish exile in New York.

Dr Gogarty survived.

He turned up at tea parties in Lady Cunard's in New York during the Second World War.

The former Maud Burke of California, relative of Robert Emmet, sung about by Count John McCormack of Athlone.

Alone in New York: Gogarty a bohemian, an autumn leaf.

He is an autumnal person.

And always there's the sea, the radiance of the sea at the Forty Foot, which he made his own and where he used swim with tempestuous regularity in his youth. And there's the bitter cold of the Liffey, the Liffey into which he jumped one winter and swam to save his life, the bitter cold of the Irish emotions that had tried to murder him.

They'd burned his library in north Connemara where the panelling had been made of the wood of shipwrecks ... Condillac, Helvétius ...

With the crow's feet of his temples, the raised, almost halter-like enclosure of hair around his temples, he drops in for an hour or so at a tea party in New York – Worcester tea service and Derby Botanical dessert service – and then he walks off, a winter swimmer remembering Dublin, the way light hit the warm-gold lettering of a pub mirror, the way radiance hit a certain joker's pub anecdote.

And somewhere in him, in these late-autumn days, is a naked young swimmer's buttocks, bruised together like the face of a young Byronesque-featured wit at a Catholic public school that had the acrid smell of shoe polish.

Yes, in these days of Fall, he remembers his brother-poet Catullus:

'What human form is there which I have not had? A woman, man, youth, boy ...'

And though it's Fall there's the urge for a swim, Coney Island maybe, the peanut whistle sounding, past the monuments to Garibaldi and to the Unknown Soldier, the Stars and Stripes fluttering over a few gentlemen swimmers who still wear the old-fashioned, black, bib top, swimming suits so that we are presented with epochs that eddy together – like the autumn and Atlantic-caressed flag.

Oystercatcher

'The American war,' the kids outside Funland, with its Jungle Jim's, its video games, snooker, pool, call it.

War where you can identify your target on tank computer screens, war fought with mobile phones.

Marshall, Sudsy's father, eyes green as the winter pastures of seaweed left on Callahane Strand, which the Atlantic enters by way of a sound, fought in the American war.

They brought him home, shot three times in the head, left eye blown away and left side of face.

Killed near the Helmand River, semi-desert land, south-west Afghanistan.

After the terrible crossing of the Gedrosian desert, en route back from India, Alexander the Great's soldiers had clapped and shouted until he kissed Bagoas, the Persian boy.

Children weren't allowed into Cross's Funeral Home in Barrack Lane, Limerick, where once there'd been a British barracks.

Marshall was from The Island, near English Town, Limerick, where Mrs Hannah Villier's almshouses for Protestant widows still stand and are used for their original purpose.

The lid of the coffin was down but it wasn't sealed so you could lift it and look at the body, and Sudsy and his friend Millsy, who had a Red Indian hairstyle like the hoopoe bird, lifted it.

'There's a man in Tralee who thinks he's Elvis Presley. He shaves his legs and wears shorts in winter,' a woman was heard to say in Cross's Funeral Home, peroxide upper-half hair, dark-chocolate bottom-half, in poison-green pumps, to a woman with blue and magenta eyeshadow.

Another story – *scéalín* – overheard: 'A dealer moved into Smudge the Dealer's patch near Funland and Smudge put a knife through both his hands and then ordered a Kerry cab to take him to the Regional Hospital.

'There are two brothels in Tralee. If you knock at the door of one a black man answers,' a man in a pinstripe jacket told a boy in a hoodie jacket so white he looked like a snow goose.

Two brothels and thirteen betting shops ...

Vigilantes – concerned parents – knock at doors on Manor Estate and Shanakill Estate to say to young dealers: 'If you're not gone in two days you'll get a beating.'

Young dealers' trailers are set aflame in the countryside. But the vigilantes – the concerned parents – are known to sell drugs themselves for profit.

Sometimes in Tralee you hear a voice like the cry of a trapped bird.

Is it a pied oystercatcher?

A one-legged oystercatcher comes every winter to the mouth of the River Lí at Trá Lí Mic Dedad – Strand of Lí, son of Dedad – coral-red bill, polar-white V shape of jet black; pink leg.

In Tralee bay you see the Orphic and stunning journeys of the grey plovers, ringed plovers, knots.

The knots still retain ravishing summer chestnut on their breasts when they arrive in August from Greenland – land of blood-red *bygds* (hamlets), which the exiled Erik the Red (subject of an Icelandic saga) failed to approach with a boat full of livestock on first attempt, because of drift ice.

Ariadne made Theseus a string of diamonds to release him from the labyrinth after he slayed the Minotaur, and the winter plovers and knots in Tralee bay look like this.

Traveller boys from a hostel in town frequently march like the Parisian sans-culottes and Marseille federalists on the Bastille or the Tuileries, on the house I live in, where I have a basement caboose.

They leave Sam Spudz Burger Bite papers; potato-snack papers; Skittles all-the-colour-of-the-rainbow papers; Calippo Strawberry Tropical drink cartons, Capri-Sun orange drink cartons.

One morning I find an electric-blue junior bicycle torn apart limb by limb outside my door.

Some nights they manage to guillotine a medium-sized palm tree, its head lying on the ground.

The river soil here was good for cider apples.

The uncle of the author of John McCormack's song, 'The Rose of Tralee', lived in this house.

His nephew fell in love with a servant girl in the house and wrote the song about her.

'The pale moon was rising ...'

John McCormack toured Australia with Nellie Melba in Italian opera.

He also toured music shops in Dublin, humming a song he heard his mother-in-law sing until the song was identified.

Now the Roses of Tralee in the Rose of Tralee Festival are pelted with rotten eggs and glass stink bombs.

Two Roses on the Chernobyl Children's Project float, one in a flowered and draped marchesa gown, the other in a butterfly gown with huge chiffon sleeves, were hit on Boherbee – the Yellow Road.

One-legged oystercatcher ...

A one-legged man used sell goods to Travellers beside the former British army living quarters, now flats.

There were British army soccer and rugby pitches nearby and Mitchel's and Kevin Barry Estates were built on them. The people of these estates are known as 'garden boys'.

'They put a fellow from Kevin Barry's Estate in jail for rape, down below, and they wouldn't let him go on top in case he'd rape someone else. He learnt how to make Gladstone bags there.'

Sudsy was outside the house one rainy evening after I'd witnessed the courtship parade of the oystercatchers on Trá Lí Mic Dedad, which was much like the Rose of Tralee parade.

Ochre-brown eyes like a snail escaped from its shell, hair alternatively red and rye bread-coloured.

He was with a blonde nymphet in a Presentation Convent tattersall maxi-skirt, just recovered from a vomiting virus that was afflicting Tralee, who was always requesting cigarettes from me near Funland although I don't smoke.

'Have you got a spare fag?'

Told me the story of his father.

In Afghani mythology there is a huge and mysterious bird, probably a heron, originally created by God, but destroyed because it had become a plague.

Melampus saved the lives of two snakes and they licked his ears while he was sleeping and he got the language of birds.

Marshall and his Tralee wife Shalina went to New York, benefitting from a wave of green cards made available to citizens of the Irish Republic.

They broke up after four years.

Shalina brought Sudsy back to Tralee, aged three.

Sudsy found out at Mounthawk School that Éamon de Valera, future prime minister of Ireland, painted by Seán Ó Sullivan in de Valera's neutral wartime Ireland in ecclesiastical-purple tie, with rounded spectacles, was aged three when his Uncle Ned Coll brought him back to Ireland from New York on the SS *City of Chicago*, carrying him over the hills from Kilmallock train station in south Limerick to nearby Bruree.

Éamon de Valera's dead Spanish father had feet so small they could fit into Éamon de Valera's immigrant mother's shoes.

But Sudsy frequently visited his father in New York.

He was photographed against the World Trade Centre, August 2001, in a lemon, horizontally striped polo shirt with a splash of sky blue at the partly buttoned section.

The following August at Ground Zero he heard how rugby

player Mark Bingham had overpowered the terrorists, preventing United Airlines Flight 93 from reaching its intended target of the White House, the plane crashing in Somerset County, south-western Pennsylvania, killing all forty-four people on board.

Sudsy took a holiday with his father at a Superstore in Florida.

Photographed against the store in wine Bermudas and his father's American army jacket.

Sudsy took a photograph of Marshall in floral-print swimming trunks, tattoo of a swallow with the message 'Rebel' in his mouth just above his navel; tattoo of a décolleté blonde fifties girl on his chest, flamingo ribbon in her hair, watermelon pink shoulder-strap dress, crowned songbirds each side of her; on his right arm a tattoo of ferocious Chinese general Sun Tzu – deeply slanted eyebrows, small instalment of beard under chin and pyramid chin-beard – got at Hanky Panky's tattoo museum in the Red Light District, Amsterdam.

Sun Tzu's words were translated by a French Jesuit, Father Amiot, shortly before the French Revolution:

All warfare is based on deception.

The supreme art of war is to subdue the enemy without fighting.

Know the enemy and know yourself.

With these admonitions Marshall went to fight in Afghanistan.

Furry clusters of spikenard in the earth, gum on myrrh-tree trunks, cedars, lilies; fields of opium poppies; blue mosques; dromedaries – post-camels; karakul – the Persian lamb – sheep with dark curled fleece; playing polo with a headless calf; dog fights; bodies on biers; women in blue burkas – full-length hooded garments; some with shawl on head, the folds of which they hold; men in sheepskin coats and Ali Baba turbans and shoes; lapis lazuli; the white spotted deer; Parnassian butterfly, translucent white wings with dark markings, red and yellow spots on hind wings.

Hadn't Bagoas played his harp of tortoiseshell and boxwood with ivory keys for Alexander the Great in this land?

Four and a half million Afghanis live in Iran – Bagoas's home country.
Good workers.

Some benefit from the off-licences they don't have in Afghanistan.
And the homemade 'Rocky' – vodka.

Death sentence meted to a 23-year-old student in Afghanistan who downloaded a report on women's rights from the Internet.

Very shortly before a young man had been executed in city of Kermanshah in Iran for the alleged rape of three boys. Accusers recanted their statements. The executed young man had testified his confession to police had been made under coercion.

Parham, the boyfriend of Mehdi Kazemi, alternatively seeking asylum in the Netherlands and England, had been hanged for sodomy in Bagoas's home country.

'The first war is better than the final friendship,' goes a Persian proverb.

A caterpillar about to break into a red admiral butterfly; starlings like raisins on a hillock; Penal Days' rabbits; the moist oracles of the curlew.

In scarlet T-shirt with lots of penguins on it, Sudsy comes to my door with the Presentation Convent girl.

He doesn't make conversation but snogs her as if for my benefit – a kind of dogging.

'What do you get when you cross a sheep with a kangaroo?' a boy with pied bandana under his baseball hat that has studs on the front of it asks me outside Funland.

'A woolly jumper.'

'What's the difference between a bird and a fly? ... A bird can fly but a fly can't bird.'

Girls in white tracksuits stand outside Funland like herring gulls about to make a short flight and whip up some morsels.

A cream-white Sein Féin van continually passes me as I cycle to see the tapestry of oystercatchers and starlings over Banna Strand or the sky dense with two hundred brent geese, with ikons of Sein Féin representatives in Marks and Spencer suits and lorikeet pink or Persian melon ties.

On 7 March 1923 Free State officers O'Daly, Clarke and Flood tied nine captured anti-Treatyites to a mine they had prepared near Ballyseedy Cross outside Tralee and blew them up, killing eight, a reprisal for the killing of five Free State soldiers with a booby-trapped landmine at Knocknagoshel the previous day, including two Dublin guards.

There'd been a seaborne invasion of anti-Treatyite Kerry at Fenit, just outside Tralee, August 1922, where the oystercatcher flies close to you on solitary journeys and the emerald-green shag continually opens its wings by Fenit's Tower of Hercules – rock-island lighthouse.

Sometimes Sudsy and his girlfriend peep in at the collage on my wall.

Caravaggio's Saint John the Baptist in the wilderness: febrile-red hair, kissing a ram, eagerly displaying sparse salami-coloured pubic hair, maraschino-cherry and pearl garments enthusiastically discarded alongside him – a stripper Saint John the Baptist.

Orazio Riminaldi's Cupid, with barbed penis, squashing books, just avoiding a mandolin – no respect for the printed word – leering above it, gloating over its destruction.

Parmigianino's Cupid: corkscrew chestnut curls, Prussian-blue wings, rosy lower buttocks as if he'd just been sitting on the potty.

Hippolyte Flandrin's urchin by the sea; nude youth in wombal position on a pistachio robe against the vitreous green sea, embracing his knees, hair en brosse, sideburns of the Second Empire, apple-red cheeks dipped toward his cloistered pubes.

A funeral solemnly enters Saint John's Parish Church and facing it are three stretch limousines, white, black, white, which have halted.

Inside are women who look like a cross between the Pussycat Dolls and Diana Ross & the Supremes.

Peekaboo hairstyles — bouffants that cover one eye. Hair blonde above, Vesuvius-red at the bottom. Frou-frou dresses. Rah-rah skirts. Poodle skirts. Tiger-stripe tops. Acid-pink tops. Honey-coloured midriffs. Diamanté hip-belts.

The oldest-looking one, in a blue sheer, round-neck blouse, asks if I'd like to take a ride.

She has Medusa hair, hair of snakes.

From the blood that sprouted from Medusa's neck after her head was cut off sprang two sons and some of these women look as if they could bear sons from their necks.

'I wears kinky underwear,' a very young one, with fake garnet necklace with further pendants on it, declares.

'Hail Mary, full of grace . . .'

And she waves flash-scarlet thongs in the face of death.

I encounter a forlorn Sudsy on Cloonbeg Terrace.

He's wearing a sky-blue jersey with a little lemon flying bird on it.

His Dawes pale-purple handmade English bicycle has just been robbed.

Traveller boys approach on bicycles like a flock of immigrant yellowhammers and an older one with cider and chestnut complexion has this to say:

'It was the Pavees, the Pikies from Mitchel's Crescent who robbed that.'

Despite the fact he spent most of his life in Mitchel's Crescent before moving to a new estate, Bruach na hAbhainn — by the river.

Bruach na hAbhainn is multinational, with many asylum seekers, those who escaped detention and forcible deportation.

An Indian boy in tracksuit bottoms with buttercup banner stripe takes a mock anal-sex position with a boy in trousers with cement and whitewash pattern, who's swooning from Dutch Gold beer, which could have been from Marcantonio Raimondi's *I Modi*, the woodcuts destroyed by Vatican decree but a samizdat of them surviving to be a vogue in Raphael's circle in Rome, reinterpreted by a German, Jean-Frédérick Maximilien de Waldeck, in the nineteenth century.

A small, simian plainclothes detective jumps out of a Toyota Silica and demands to see my sketchbook.

Four-letter words stream from him.

There's another plainclothes detective in the car, an elephant in a V-necked Penneys jersey.

It's the second time this has happened to me in the Tralee area.

I am suspected of sketching male nudes.

Unsatisfied with what he finds on me he swoops on the purse containing my flat key the way the blue-tailed kestrel, who occupies abandoned crows' nests, swoops on prey in the dunes.

This happens beside the public library where they have Luca Signorelli's sketch of a nude Antaeus, giant of Libya, and a nude Hercules, who as a baby strangled the two serpents Zeus's sister-wife Hera sent to kill him, both with powerful calf muscles.

Antaeus, on touching the earth, his mother, even in wrestling combat had his strength renewed.

Palingenesis in Tralee …

In Afghanistan the Taliban, when in power, demolished two ancient statues of Buddha carved into the mountains near Bamian.

'There's a fellow in Mitchel's Crescent. He's not from there. He was in jail and he's out. He's driving them mad. Getting them to slash tyres. Burn cars.'

A torcher on Mitchel's Crescent with melted azure eyes and hair like the golden apples Hercules procured from the tree guarded by the three daughters of Hesperus, the evening star, and by Ladon, the dragon, on the world's western edge.

His *minet* – pretty boy – accomplices have High-King-of-Ireland ginger hair and wear estate baseball hats.

On 2 June 2005 Terence Wheelock, aged twenty, was arrested with three others in Dublin in connection with stealing a car.

Found unconscious later that day in Store Street garda station.

Gardaí claimed he hanged himself with a string from his tracksuit bottoms secured to a fixture countersunk in the wall. There was blood staining on his clothing inconsistent with this type of suicide.

He was taken to the Mater Hospital where he died on 16 September.

When his solicitor came to inspect the cell he'd been found unconscious in, to her dismay, it had already been renovated.

A seventeen-year-old, doing his Leaving Certificate, is found by his mother, hanging in the garage.

Six foot two – Michelangelo's super-teenager Ganymede.

Went to the Debs ball with a girl in a blue chiffon strap-dress who put stories out about his lack of sexual prowess.

Goaded by his fellow pupils at school.

Didn't soccer star Justin Fashanu hang himself from the rafters of a Shoreditch garage, with an electric flex, after a Maryland teenage boy, same age as the Kerry boy who had just hanged himself, accused him of sexual assault?

In a car park, gardaí harass Traveller boys selling holly from Killarney National Park where the azaleas are now having a second flowering, the viburnum is in blossom three months prematurely, the squirrels are still romping around the abbey where Eoghan Ruadh Ó Súilleabháin – fatally struck on the head with a tongs by the coachman of Colonel Daniel Cronin because of a satiric poem he wrote about his master – is buried.

In Baghdad, where children are sold to criminal gangs to be sexually abused, a US army sniper accused of killing an unarmed Iraqi and planting an AK-47 on his body is found guilty.

There's another war – a war against suburbia, against television, against computers, and the death toll is astronomical.

Sudsy is found to be suffering from acute leukaemia – immature white blood cells multiply rapidly, the number of normal cells decrease sharply.

An adolescent's disease.

Many in Hiroshima and Nagasaki suffered from it because of radiation exposure.

Sudsy has to get chemotherapy to kill the cancer cells and radiation therapy with high-energy X-rays, so his hair is shaven off.

The hoodie jackets multiply — a black one with a scarlet border to its hood, a cerulean one, a vertical-blue-stripe one, a paisley pattern one, a black spaghetti pattern one, a magpie one, a pinstripe one, even a silver-wash one.

'They do it on the spur of the moment. They don't know what they're doing.'

Before he puts on the toga virilis — adult toga — of his seventeenth year, Sudsy hangs himself from a stairway on a street where five gardaí live and is thus crime-free and is buried in Old Rath — pronounced Rah.

The black guillemot does not make a nest and changes to white in winter, and an albino blackbird sings near Sudsy's grave.

I meet Sudsy's girlfriend outside Funland.

She's wearing a black top that looks as if it was made out of bin-liner material.

'I had a dream about him. He said he'd meet me in my next dream.'

Then she puts headphones back on and listens to Sean Kingston — rhythm and beat, new-age reggae.

A Rumanian woman in a blue polka-dot *balzo* — turban-like hat — approaches both of us: 'I am a poor woman.'

Funland … bells and whistles, millennial logos, baseball hats, woollen hats, baseball hats sideaways, thinkaways, megabytes, something listless, something unhappy; a surfeit of technology, most of the faces on Bebo or Facebook — Sudsy's was too — a deficit of love and friendship.

There's a lot of sex.

But love … what is this love? What is this word?

I heard it once.

Acknowledgments

The author acknowledges receipt of Carlyle Membership, supported by the London Library.

These pieces have appeared in the following publications:

'Belle', *New Writing 14*, Volume 14, selected by Lavinia Greenlaw and Helon Habila (London: The British Council in association with Granta Publications, first published in Great Britain by Granta Books 2006); *The Clifden Anthology*, ed. Brendan Flynn (Clifden: Clifden Community Arts Festival 2007).

'Iowa', *The London Magazine*, ed. Sebastian Barker (February/March 2005); *Southword 12*, ed. Jon Boilard (June 2007).

'Red Tide', *The Faber Book of Best New Irish Short Stories 2006–7*, ed. David Marcus (London: Faber and Faber 2007).

'Little Friends', *The London Magazine*, ed. Sebastian Barker (October/November 2006).

'Shelter', *The London Magazine*, ed. Sebastian Barker; *Island* (February/March 2005); *Island* (Summer 2006).

'Sweet Marjoram', *The London Magazine*, ed. Sebastian Barker (April/May 2007).

'The Hare's Purse', *Cyphers*, No. 63, eds Leland Bardwell, Eileén Ní Chuilleanáin, Pearse Hutchinson, Macdara Woods (April 2007); *American Short Fiction*, Issue 38, eds Stacey Swann, Jill Meyers, Rebecca Bengal (Summer 2007).

'The House of Mourning', *Cyphers*, No. 65, eds Leland Bardwell, Eileén Ní
　　Chuilleanáin, Pearse Hutchinson, Macdara Woods (May 2008).
'Essex Skipper', *A Casualty of War: The Arcadia Book of Gay Stories*, ed. Peter
　　Burton (Arcadia Books 2008).
'Old Swords', *The Stinging Fly*, Issue 10, Volume Two, ed. Declan Meade
　　(Summer 2008).